ilence ruled the courtyard. Windows were smashed, paving ripped up, the central fountain was befouled, but worst of all, Ember's fellows lay dead. The destruction and horror were so complete that she half expected to hear echoes of the violence that had raged there, but heard only the splashing fountain and her beating heart.

Ember was strong. Her spirit was fierce and at the same time more disciplined than most others, even other members of her own order. The sight before her, however, was too much, too terrible, too extreme. Brek Gorunn barely caught the monk as she fell, senseless and despairing.

From the creators of the
greatest roleplaying game ever
come tales of heroes fighting
monsters with magic!

By T.H. Lain

OATH OF NERULL

T.H. Lain

OATH OF NERULL

Distributed in the United States by Holtzbrinck Publishing.
Distributed in Canada by Fenn Ltd.

Distributed to the hobby, toy, and comic trade in the United States and Canada by regional distributors.

Distributed worldwide by Wizards of the Coast, Inc. and regional distributors.

Cover art by Todd Lockwood
First Printing: September 2002
Library of Congress Catalog Card Number: 2002108460

9 8 7 6 5 4 3 2 1

US ISBN: 0-7869-2851-4
UK ISBN: 0-7869-2852-2
620-88240-001-EN

U.S., CANADA,	EUROPEAN HEADQUARTERS
ASIA, PACIFIC, & LATIN AMERICA	Wizards of the Coast, Belgium
Wizards of the Coast, Inc.	P.B. 2031
P.O. Box 707	2600 Berchem
Renton, WA 98057-0707	Belgium
+1-800-324-6496	+32-70-23-32-77

Visit our web site at **www.wizards.com**

Living Dead-ications

For Dee.

Catacomb Map Fragment

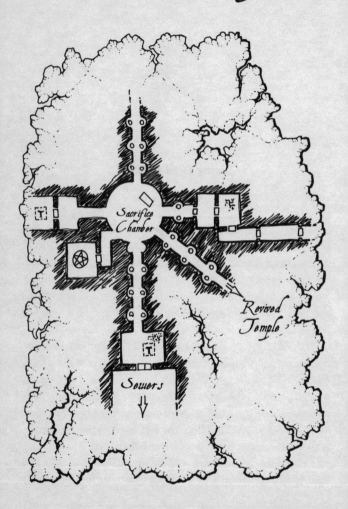

Sacrifice
Chamber

Revived
Temple

Sewers

I

The blow was vicious. Ember's sight blurred in rainbow agony as she struggled to keep her footing on the suddenly rolling pavement. A man in a red half-mask stood before her, grinning as he readied another blow. He'd come from nowhere.

Caught off guard, Ember struck back reflexively with *shi kune*, the "stunning fist." The shock of a strike traveled from her hand up her arm, telling her she'd hit something. Because of the haze behind her eyes, she couldn't be certain whether it was her ambusher or the nearby wall.

The darkness disgorged another figure. Red-masked, the figure collided with her companion, Brek Gorunn the dwarf. Despite the drumbeat of pain, she heard the grunt and clatter when the dwarf was bowled over by his assailant. She knew Brek was not nimble, and his chain mail overcoat was a heavy burden.

Warm liquid trickled into her left eye—blood, of course. Ember wondered if it was her own or her attacker's.

She shook away both stars and blood and took stock: She and Brek fought five people in red masks, purpose unknown, in a cobblestone alley. The night sky was dark under low clouds, with no moon. It was an ambush. Their attackers, whoever they were, had hoped to overwhelm her and the dwarf before they could react.

Too bad. I'm ready now, thought Ember.

One red-masked attacker lay at her feet, stunned or dying. Surprise or not, Ember was well trained in the martial arts of hand, fist, and foot. Her reflexive blow had brought her first attacker down.

Another man in a red half-mask sneered and rushed forward, executing a series of whirling strikes. She affected *bahng ah jah se*, the right guarding stance, and deflected two open-handed attacks and one elbow. Melting from guarding to offensive stance, she caught the retreating elbow with one hand and delivered a hammer blow to his elbow joint with her off hand. The man fell back with a cry. His arm hung loosely from the elbow, the joint shattered. Ember allowed herself a grim smile.

Brek Gorunn grappled with his assailant. Brek uttered a battle cry, pious by dwarf standards; Brek was an adherent of the dwarf god Moradin. The red mask's arms were wrapped around the dwarf's chest, preventing Brek from drawing his iron-shod warhammer.

Ember decided the dwarf could handle one red mask, and moved to block two others rushing forward. The dwarf could handle one, maybe, but not three at once.

"Kill them, kill them, kill them!" screamed a voice from the darkness. The voice was thin, piping, and alien.

Who . . . what said that? thought Ember, as she peered through the darkened alley.

Two figures resolved in the gloom, both similarly hidden under red masks. One continued to advance, weaponless, his stance suspiciously similar to her own. The other remained behind, observing. Something squirmed on his back—a sack?

The advancing ambusher charged. The thin voice laughed, a cacophony of splintering wood.

Ember shifted to *cha riut*, the attention stance, hoping to deflect the brunt of the attack. The snarling man still managed to land a kick to Ember's forehead. Pain blossomed like a poisonous flower. She grunted, reeled, and avoided a fall through iron determination.

"Yes! Death to the Enabled Hand! I am the Child, and I command it!" screeched the voice, almost certainly issuing from the bulging sack on the last red mask's back.

Through her pain, Ember wondered who the "child" was and why it hated her?

Brek Gorunn broke from his attacker's hold, scrambling to his feet. His enchanted warhammer fell firmly into his grip.

"You made a mistake with us, bandits. Hide your faces all you want. You can't escape Moradin's justice . . . *oof!*" Brek's attacker landed a whirling kick to the dwarf's midsection, but the dwarf remained on his feet. He looked over to Ember, and gasped "Ember, are you hurt?"

Ember waved one hand reassuringly, hoping she didn't look as bad as she felt. Weakness pulled against her every move like unseen spiderwebs. She had to end this fight quickly. Ember struck with her left hand, drawing on all her training. It was the *ah sang bo*, the swaying snake feint. Her attacker took the bait and shifted to block; Ember spun in the opposite direction and chopped his neck with her other hand. The red mask fell without a sound.

Brek Gorunn's attacker realized the tide had turned. He twisted to run. Brek roared, and his warhammer caught the man once, twice, thrice . . . and he, too, was down. The last ambusher, the one with the passenger on his back, turned and shot off down the alley. The goading voice screamed out defiantly, then faded into the distance.

The dwarf cleric gave chase, but stopped short when he saw how hurt Ember actually was. For her part, Ember felt like a glass shot through with tiny cracks. One more hit, and she'd shatter. She slowly sat down, breathing through her mouth.

Looking at her friend, she said slowly, "Brek . . . I have the feeling those were not simple bandits."

"No? Why not?" said the dwarf, as he moved back to look after Ember's hurts. He rammed his warhammer back into his wide belt, and examined Ember's wounds with a clinical air.

Ember said, "Didn't you hear that voice? 'Death to the Enabled hand,' it said. The Enabled Hand is my monastic order. Too specific for a random gang of city ruffians. And that thing riding the back of the last one. It was otherworldly."

Ember grimaced around her pains as she spoke.

"Yes, I suppose you're right," said Brek, distracted.

Ember recognized the distraction—the monk presumed that Brek was visualizing his connection to the divine. With the right prayer, his became the hands of a healer, mediating the grace of Moradin.

The dwarf chanted a short prayer, and where he touched, Ember's wounds healed as if they'd never been . . . all except for a headache that was determined to remain.

So be it, thought Ember, as my old instructor Kairoth said so often, "pain is weakness leaving the body."

New strength grew in her, welling up from a hidden reserve and from the healing power of Brek.

"So, you think these red-masked ambushers are connected to the troubles of the Enabled Hand?" wondered the dwarf.

Ember reflected. The Enabled Hand had several chapters. Her chapter was here in the city of Volanth. Of late, the chapter's luck was down. First that terrible fire, then the thefts. Recently, monks had gone missing. That was when the order hired Brek Gorunn to investigate with her. Brek was a long-time friend of the order. The dwarf felt that Moradin's work coincided with the interests of the Hand. She and Brek were checking a clue concerning one of the missing monks when they were attacked.

"I don't know, but I wonder. I do know one thing."

"What's that?"

"We should return to the chapter house. I have a bad feeling," said Ember. She stood, flexing her arms. Her pallor faded, leaving her skin its normal shade of ebony. She walked up to a fallen red mask, the one whose arm she'd broken. He still lived. She bent down and removed his mask. Below the red covering, his face seemed normal, unremarkable.

"I wonder if these fellows are responsible for the missing monks. If we hadn't been stronger, we would have gone missing, too. Why the red masks, and who are they working for?"

The unconscious man told no tales, for now.

Ember continued, "I noticed something else very troubling. The ambushers were proficient in the art of the hand, foot, and fist, the same as we teach in my order. How do you explain that?"

"A rival monastery?" offered Brek.

The dwarf's face creased in thought. His fingers tapped a silent rhythm on his warhammer, his weapon and holy symbol to Moradin the Dwarffather.

Ember shook her head, frowning, and said, "I can't recall any rival. If we have such a rival, it is new." The monk turned back to the ambusher with the broken arm. "Help me with this one. The master instructor can question him."

So saying, she grabbed a limp arm, unconcerned that it was the broken one, and Brek Gorunn grabbed the other. They carried their unconscious prisoner down the alley and out onto the street.

Volanth, a trade city, was unremarkable in its architecture. Simple, one-story wooden buildings were the rule. In the residential section, where Ember and Brek were attacked, all was dark save for a few buildings that showed lights behind drawn shades. The Enabled Hand chapter house, their destination, was located on a street called Bridge Place, a walk of little more than a quarter mile. Ember and Brek moved briskly despite their unconscious burden. As in any city, many people were abroad by night, though few paid them any heed. Those who noticed the trio assumed that the human woman and dwarf were helping an intoxicated friend home after a too-boisterous celebration in a local tavern.

As they walked, Ember's disquiet grew. She should have reported back to the chapter house earlier. They had been too busy, too close to what they thought was a lead. Instead of them finding it, the lead had found them.

When they sighted the chapter house, Ember's uncertain feelings woke into outright alarm. Normally, a golden lamp shone above the main entrance. There was no glow now. The lamp was smashed. Ember dropped the arm of the captive and ran forward.

"Ember, be careful!" cautioned the dwarf.

But she was beyond caring. She rushed into the building, past an open door that should have been closed and locked.

Inside, she found a slaughter.

"By the Dwarffather, they are worsted," murmured Brek Gorunn.

The dwarf cleric moved up alongside Ember. She stared in stunned silence. Distantly, she wondered if Brek had secured their captive.

Silence ruled the courtyard. Windows were smashed, paving ripped up, the central fountain was befouled, but worst of all, Ember's fellows lay dead. The destruction and horror were so complete that she half expected to hear echoes of the violence that had raged there, but heard only the splashing fountain and her beating heart.

Ember was strong. Her spirit was fierce and at the same time more disciplined than most others, even other members of her own order. The sight before her, however, was too much, too terrible, too extreme. Brek Gorunn barely caught the monk as she fell, senseless and despairing.

Ember woke, but kept her eyes closed. Her head still pained her, but a hollow, deeper ache pulsed through her. Why? For a second, she could not remember. It lasted just that second, and when it passed, she wished she could call that precious moment back.

One thing was clear to her. If she was to survive, emotionally, she must harden her spirit. She must quiet her heart-loss, for now, to discover who was behind the atrocity.

Fainting damsels may be something commoners expect, but I will have no more of it, she mentally vowed.

Spurred by this thought, Ember drew her new resolve around her like a cloak, opened her eyes, and looked around.

Brek Gorunn had been busy—she must have lain unconscious for a few hours. The worst of the horror was cleared away so that she was not immediately faced with the sight of her slain compatriots. She owed the dwarf a debt of gratitude for that kindness. She lay on folded tapestries, apparently procured from a nearby wall by Brek. Near her, the captive ambusher lay securely trussed.

His mask was missing, and his face glared back at Ember with undisguised hate, but he said nothing.

Ember rose, called, "Brek?"

Hearing no answer for the moment, she approached the captive. He continued to glare.

Ember told him, "I suppose you know we intend to find out who you are. You might as well tell me now. Brek Gorunn, my dwarf friend, will not be so merciful as I."

Ember knew neither she nor Brek would stoop to the tactics of evil, but hoped the bluff would have some effect.

It did not. The man just glared.

Ember approached closer, thinking that perhaps she wasn't only bluffing after all.

"The pain you visited upon those here will be returned to you threefold if you do not speak, *now!*" she yelled, ending with all her volume.

The man's glare gave way to uncertainty. She had him. He knew that she was not the sort to make idle threats.

The captive opened his mouth, and she saw what she had not seen before. The man had no tongue. He would not tell her or anyone anything. Ember shook her head and moved away. She restrained herself from kicking him, though she wanted to desperately.

Instead she looked at the man and said, "You are not worth it. Do you know why? Because cruelty is a tool for the weak."

Looking around again, she called to Brek once more. This time the dwarf appeared from an antechamber, wiping his hands on another piece of shredded tapestry.

"Ember, I'm so sorry. I . . ." The dwarf was at a loss for words.

She shook her head. "Brek, if I am to get through this, mourning will follow after. Right now, we must get to the bottom of the attack. And he—" she pointed to the mute captive—"is useless."

Brek nodded. "He and his friends did seem awfully quiet when we were attacked, except for that one awful voice. Now we know why."

The monk pondered a moment then said, "The red masks' plans may not be limited to the Volanth chapter house of the Enabled Hand. The threat called out by that 'child' did not limit itself to only Volanth. My warning came too late, here, to my eternal shame. But there is something I can do to make up for that. I need to travel immediately to the Motherhouse of the Enabled Hand, to the root of our order. They must be warned. At the very least, I need to report what was done here. I owe that to Kairoth."

Brek raised an eyebrow. "Your old instructor?"

"Yes, him." In fact, Ember had received a letter from Kairoth only the day before. Ember carried Kairoth's letter in her satchel. She and her teacher had maintained friendly correspondence over the years. Kairoth was *sa bum nim*, an honored instructor in the Motherhouse. He sat with the elders of the Enabled Hand. In his letter, he wrote, among other things, about the recent Day of Fasting. "Kairoth will know what to do, if anyone."

The dwarf said, "You've told me stories about him. Anyhow, what about the local authorities—the Volanth Watch should be contacted."

Ember paused for a moment, then continued. "If we involve the Volanth Watch, valuable time will be lost. A day at least, as we testify to the magistrate—possibly a week. I need to be on the road today toward the Motherhouse in New Koratia. The elders must be warned. We can't spare time here."

"The city of New Koratia is a good distance," mused Brek Gorunn. "But of course the warning must be made. Allow me to join you on the road. After all, I was attacked by these red-masked men while I was in the employ of the order. Plus, Moradin's ire has been pricked," concluded the dwarf, his face grim.

Ember allowed herself a look of gratitude. "Then, let's gather what stories we can from the destruction here, and move out. I suppose I should retrieve the gems in the chapter house treasury and bring them to the Motherhouse."

Brek sighed. "Ember, the treasury is looted. I looked around while you lay asleep. The vault is open and empty."

The monk closed her eyes but said nothing. She mentally moved into the *gunnun so gee* posture, the walking stance, drawing calm from its strength.

"But," continued Brek, "I also found this. It explains much, while raising even more questions." He produced a small ring. It bore the insignia of a skull and sickle. "I recognize this symbol," Brek said. "It is the sign of the death god Nerull, called the Hater of Life, the Reaper of Flesh, and other more terrible names."

Ember looked up, startled. "But the last of Nerull's priests were unmasked and ejected from civilized lands years ago. How could this be?"

Brek nodded. "Nerull-worship was banned, yes, but banning something doesn't erase it. Especially Nerull. His is an evil that does not sleep. Nerull and those who revere him remain in the world, hidden, however much we comfort ourselves by thinking otherwise."

The dwarf squeezed the ring hard, and continued, "This ring proves that at least one of those who attacked the chapter, if not all, owe their allegiance to the Hater of Life. All the more reason to find out who they are and where they nest, so we can stamp them out."

"Very well," Ember sighed. "A banished cult has killed my chapter and looted the treasury. Still, there may be something they didn't get . . . something the order may need. It would do no good to leave anything of significance here."

So saying, Ember walked to the edge of the fountain.

The basin was carved from green-veined marble. In it stood a statue of a man carved from the same block of stone. He wore loose clothing, not unlike Ember's own dress, and stood in a ready stance, palms upward and slightly cupped. It was from his cupped hands that water spilled to splash into the wide basin.

Ember studied the fountain and said, "This is Loku, the founder of this chapter. He was a great warrior. The chapter honors him, as does the whole order. Did you know he once saved the Motherhouse from destruction? So say the histories. We keep no relics in the strict sense of the word, but we do treasure one of Loku's cast-off possessions. It was kept here, hidden in the fountain."

The monk walked into the basin. Bloody water splashed around her ankles. She knelt and reached into the murk, groping for a hidden mechanism.

"Ah, here it is."

Brek Gorunn, watching Ember, said, "Ember, there's something else you should know. It's about some of the monks' bodies I cleared away. A few were . . . melted. No, that's not the best word for it. They were dissolved, as if acid or some corrosive, alchemical mixture had been poured on them."

Ember did not pause in her activity, but her breath caught and her eyes narrowed. "Then, they shall pay all the more."

She didn't want to hear the dwarf's words, so she concentrated on finding the second catch to the secret vault in the fountain. A rush of bubbles marked her success. Ember extended her hand into the cavity below the waterline and yanked. With a click, two panels popped open in the arms of the sculpture. Inside each hidden recess lay a leather arm band. The bracers were pristine, and in fact seemed to glisten with a faint, golden light. The woman lifted the bracers out and held them up.

"These are Loku's Bracers. By taking them from this reliquary,

I symbolically disperse the Volanth order of the Enabled Hand. And so it is done; Volanth chapter is no more."

"What are you going to do with them?"

"Wear them, of course. They are woven round with spells of defense. I expect I shall need their protection on the road to New Koratia." Ember strapped the bracers on and stepped across the basin's edge. "I don't think Loku will mind, since I'm the only member of the chapter remaining."

Wearing the bracers, Ember felt emboldened, magnified. The dwarf looked at her with admiration. Ember wondered whether the relics should have seen the light of day earlier. Perhaps if someone had worn them, instead of locking them away, the tragedy might have been averted. On her arms, the bracers felt as if they had been custom made for her.

Brek cautioned, "I know you want to get started immediately, but we both need rest, after all. Let's sleep for what remains of the night anyway, then leave at dawn."

"Agreed. New Koratia can wait those few hours."

"You think so? Then watch!" said the small man—or, more precisely, said the gnome.

These small-statured, nimble-fingered folk made up for their lack in size with enthusiasm. At least this gnome did. He wore an elaborate coat with many pockets, and goggles pushed up on his forehead. His name was Nebin Raulnor, and he was explaining the superiority of his craft to his friend, Hennet. Nebin and Hennet shared a table in a roadside tavern called the Fair Warrior.

Hennet was a young, human male from the distant east. His dress, barbaric by civilized standards, consisted of leather leggings, spiked bracers, a wide belt, and a suitably dramatic cloak. Two entwined dragons were tattooed on his chest. Hennet, like Nebin, was also a student of the craft, though he came at it from a far different direction than the gnome. Their differences, often enough rubbing both the wrong way, were in truth the bond that continually strengthened their easy camaraderie.

Nebin screwed up his face, as if recalling something complex. The gnome chanted a few unintelligible syllables, gesticulating with his hands. Called by his arcane manipulations, a ten-foot ball of red fire appeared in the center of the tavern. It burned like a piece of Hell itself, though it made no sound.

Hennet watched the display with a single, raised eyebrow. The other tavern patrons reacted less calmly. There was a stifled scream, many shouts, and the crashing of overturned chairs. Cries of "Fire!" brought the taverner from the kitchen, a bucket of water in one hand. He hurled the bucket, and the water passed through the globe of fire as if it wasn't there. And a second later, it wasn't.

"By Pelor's blinding eyes, who's working magic in my house?" bellowed the taverner. He glared around the room.

Someone in back murmured, "It was only shadow magic. Any fool could see that."

Another patron laughed, if a bit nervously. A few people hadn't even stood, including those at the table where Hennet and Nebin sat. The gnome ducked his head.

At still another table, a dwarf in a mail overcoat scowled. The dwarf's companion, a capable-looking human woman wearing a travel-stained cloak, returned to her meal as if the sudden appearance of balls of flame was commonplace. Hennet was struck by her easy manner. Soon enough, everyone returned to their seats, righting chairs and laughing at the prankster, who-ever he was.

The taverner sighed and returned to the kitchen. As he moved from sight, he yelled, "the Fair Warrior is a tavern, not a carnival. No more magic, or you'll be out on your butts!"

Nebin peered after the retreating taverner and said, "Again, I've demonstrated the advantage of wizardry, Hennet. That was a minor spell, but with it I create the image of anything I can imag-ine. That's just one of the many wonders I have recorded here." Nebin patted a heavy, metal-bound book he carried on a shoul-der strap.

The young man scratched his chin. "A wonder? More a spectacle. Of course I've seen you pull that one off before. You're lucky the taverner didn't see you. I doubt I'd have stood up for you. It is cold out tonight."

The sorcerer laughed, and Nebin sniffed.

"Him? I doubt he'd trifle with someone of my obvious talents."

Hennet smiled as they settled into one of their favorite arguments.

He said, "Besides, you've just admitted your weakness. Once you have expended your magic, you're no different from anyone else. You have to return to your book of spells to study, or be completely bereft of enchantment. But me? Once I master a particular piece of the craft, I never forget. It becomes part of me, and I, it."

Nebin chuckled. "So you say. True, you never consult a spellbook. But, be honest, it's no secret that raw workers of the craft, such as yourself, are limited to only a few spells. We've been together a long time now, and I can see it's true. Take me, on the other hand. I'm only limited by what I can scribe in this book."

Again, the gnome patted his metal-bound tome.

It was one of Nebin's favorite gestures. Hennet thought it was the most annoying in an extended list of habits, all of which were annoying to various degrees. Despite that, Hennet liked the gnome and considered him a friend. Trading barbs was one of their favorite pastimes, and on the road to attend the Duel Arcane, it was expected.

Neither Hennet nor Nebin had previously attended the Duel Arcane, held in New Koratia every three years. Both knew of it for years, though, and had thought about it since taking up studying the craft, each after his own fashion. The Duel Arcane was the most prestigious magical competition in the region. Merely attending the event was an honor. They were both nervous, but neither would admit that to the other. At least Hennet wouldn't—

he wasn't entirely sure if Nebin's bravado was real or feigned. Their arguments, with their bluster and straightforward hauteur, helped to keep nervousness at bay.

Hennet looked back at the gnome. Nebin had been speaking, but Hennet wasn't sure of the topic. To rattle his friend, Hennet broke in, interrupting the gnome's speech.

"Nebin," he said, "I've been meaning to ask you—do those even do anything?"

Hennet waved a finger at the goggles the gnome wore pushed up onto his forehead. It was the gnome's habit (another one) to pull them down over his eyes when he faced a dangerous situation.

Nebin paused mid-speech, looked vaguely disturbed, then continued where he had left off, ignoring Hennet's question altogether.

Hennet grinned, trying to take in the gnome's point. It was the classic sorcerer versus wizard argument, something they'd talked to death many times. By round-about fashion, the gnome would imply that sorcerers like Hennet could never truly experience the wonder a wizard (such as the gnome) felt upon discovering a new spell and scribing it into his spellbook.

To forestall another pat on the book, Hennet interrupted his friend once more, but this time with a serious question: "Do you think either of us has a chance at winning the Golden Wand?"

The prize awarded at the conclusion of a Duel Arcane was highly coveted, even though it was awarded only to mages competing as novices. The prize earned by experienced mages was a closely guarded secret, known only to those who had won. Both Hennett and Nebin expected to someday learn for themselves. For now, the Golden Wand was their goal.

"It should be a snap," said Nebin, displaying his characteristic overconfidence. "Though I apologize in advance for taking that honor from you, my friend."

Nebin laughed good-naturedly, showing his statement was meant as a joke. Hennet joined in, then finished his drink.

After more talk about the competition, the two mages retired to their shared room. Neither was flush with cash, and the city of New Koratia, where the duel was to be held, would be expensive.

The Fair Maiden had a second story filled with clean rooms set aside for travelers. That nightnight, all the rooms were filled, so they felt lucky not to be camping alongside the road, as they had done too many times in the past.

Nebin shrugged out of his coat and kicked off his boots, then took to his cot immediately. Hennet sat on his cot, boots off and legs folded, and began his nightly reflection before sleep. He mentally examined secrets of power and magic he knew, and used those secrets to probe for deeper secrets that lay latent within him. Most nights, he came away with nothing, but not always. Sometimes a new insight, a new twist on old knowledge, blossomed under his inner scrutiny. Such was the way of sorcery. Soon enough, he would drift into sleep, perhaps with a tiny, new coal of arcane power smoldering at the back of his mind.

A noise woke Nebin from sound sleep. He cocked his head, listening for it again—nothing. He smiled, all too familiar with the figments of his mind. Then he frowned. He was sure he heard something scratching at the door.

What an unnerving possibility, he thought. Should I check to make sure? I'll never get to sleep otherwise, the gnome realized.

He considered waking Hennet, but decided against it. If it was nothing, he would only have disturbed his friend's rest.

Better to check first, Nebin decided.

The gnome's fingers trailed across his spellbook as he quietly slipped from bed. He'd cast one of his spells earlier, and it would take too long to renew it. Contrary to what he'd told Hennet, the enchantment he'd loosed earlier in the tavern's common room was one of his most potent illusions. He always felt a little naked without its subtle presence in the back of his mind.

The gnome minced across the cold floor toward the door. With his small stature and without his leather boots, he made no sound. The door was bolted on the inside. Nebin listened for just a moment, making sure the hall was silent, then he drew the bolt back, pulling it so slowly he could barely see it move. He pulled the door toward himself until a sliver of black appeared between it and the jamb. The hallway, which would have looked black as pitch to Hennett's human eyes, stood out in dim but distinct outlines to the gnome. Nebin's problem was that, peering through the tiny crack, he could see less than half the hallway. Most of it extended the opposite direction.

Mustering his nerve, he eased the door open wider and slipped his head through the opening into the hall. He quickly scanned both directions. Three small skylights allowed waning moonlight into the corridor, casting soft, almost imperceptible shadows. Nebin could see a blot at the far end of the hallway, but in that near-total darkness, even he could not make out what it was. A large pack, perhaps? Nebin briefly wondered if one of the inn's patrons, having drunk too much wine, eaten too little food, or simply walked too many miles, might have dropped a big, bulging sack and forgotten it.

The more he stared at it, however, the more he questioned whether it really was a pack. It looked more like a sack.

No, not a sack, he thought, but a very, very large cocoon. But that was ridiculous.

With thoughts of giant cocoons in his head, Nebin's heart skipped a beat when the object suddenly appeared to shift.

Is it moving, he wondered? Is it . . . looking at me?

Nebin uttered a whispery squeak and snapped back into his room. In his fright, he banged his ear on the door frame, jammed his thumb as he pushed the bolt home, and stubbed his toe leaping into bed. He rolled in his blanket, shivering and gazing at the door with large, unblinking eyes. Nebin did not like that sack. He didn't believe he would ever like any sack that had eyes.

Hennet continued to sleep, undisturbed.

Seconds turned to minutes, and the silence remained unbroken.

Maintaining terror in the absence of threat, real or imagined, is a chore. Gradually the gnome convinced himself that he had seen only a discarded sack after all. It wouldn't be the first time his imagination conjured frightful things in the night. It was a good thing he hadn't awakened Hennett, he decided. The sorcerer would have enjoyed a good laugh at the gnome's expense—frightened by a sack! Finally, white-knuckled, sheet-clutching fingers relaxed and shivering gave way to snoring. Nebin's sleep was untroubled the rest of the night.

A scream, loud and shrill, roused the guests of the Fair Warrior at dawn.

Hennet jumped from his bed. He grabbed his cape for a robe and dashed for the door. Nebin sat up bleary-eyed, questioning.

"Hennet, are you going out for breakfast?"

Hennet shook his head and stepped into the hallway.

He hissed back at Nebin, "There's trouble, be ready!"

A few other groggy travelers milled about, and more exited

into the hallway from their rooms looking as disheveled as Hennett. The largest group stood near a door at the end of the hall. A small, human woman pushing a cleaning cart was crying loudly. People were comforting her. Hennet pushed his way through the press. No one hindered him, and he peered into the far room. It was another guest room, very much like his own—except for the body.

A woman lay half-on, half-off her cot. She was clearly dead. Her left leg was missing from mid-thigh on down. What remained of the stump was tattered and charred, as if it had somehow been melted away. Hennet felt bile rising in his throat, so he turned away. Looking back down the hallway toward his own room, he saw Nebin gazing out with wide eyes. The sorcerer shook his head sadly and made a slashing motion across his neck. Nebin's eyes narrowed to slits.

He doesn't seem surprised, mused Hennet.

Like so many of the wizard's mannerisms and habits, this one was well known to the sorcerer. The gnome knew something about this murder.

Ember, Brek Gorunn, and their captive made good time after leaving Volanth, hiking along a well-traveled road toward New Koratia. The Fair Warrior Inn was a welcome respite to camping along the road. Ember shared a room with Brek and their captive for security. But in the morning, a scream disturbed Ember's sleep.

She rose from her cot, reaching smoothly for her sandals. One was laced up before she realized that Brek was gone. And the prisoner was gone, too! Ember uttered an oath and laced up her remaining sandal in record time, then dashed into the corridor outside the room. Several people stood near the end of the hallway.

If Brek rose early, she wondered, why would he leave and take the prisoner with him?

A dark-haired man in a cape stood in an open doorway. He signaled to someone past Ember's room, a sleepy-eyed but scared gnome standing in the doorway of another guest room near the opposite end of the hallway. There was only one way to interpret the gesture; someone had died.

Ember called the dark-haired man. "You, with the cape! What's going on?"

The man looked at her, glanced back into the room, then moved up to stand next to her. She noticed his bare feet and legs, plus an interesting tattoo of two dragons on his chest.

"I am Hennet," said the caped man. "I'm afraid there is a murderer among us. A woman lies dead in that room. And she died by unnaturally cruel means. She looks partly melted." The man hesitated as he spoke this last bit, obviously unsettled.

Ember stiffened at the news. She pushed past Hennet to take a look herself. At her back, she heard the taverner tramping up the stairs, yelling for guests to return to their rooms. Ember paid him no mind. In the room, she saw the scene described by Hennet.

She'd half hoped to also find Brek Gorunn (but, gods preserve, not as the victim). Brek spoke of those slain in her own order as partly dissolved as if by alchemical acid—the similarity of this woman's condition couldn't be a simple coincidence.

Where has that dwarf gotten to? she wondered.

The taverner looked into the room and told Ember, "Clear out! The authorities are on their way."

Ember didn't care to see the grisly scene any longer, anyway. She left the room and accosted the taverner. "Has anything like this happened before?" she asked.

Ember noticed that most of the guests were returning to their rooms, happy to let someone else deal with the problem. Only the caped man, Hennet, and his friend the gnome remained interested.

The taverner gave Ember an appraising look. "Happened before? Of course not. What an idea!" he said, rubbing his nose nervously.

Ember continued, "Fine. Have you seen my companion out

and about this morning? You remember, the dwarf I arrived with last night? It is unsettling to find a murder and a missing person on the same morning—I'm worried about him."

Hennet moved to stand closer to the taverner, fixing him with a penetrating look, and a few beads of sweat broke out on the man's brow.

"Why ask me? I haven't seen your dwarf friend or anyone else this morning. I just woke up. Perhaps he went outside for a breath of air." The taverner rubbed his nose again. Ember tried to meet his gaze, but the man stared determinedly at the door to the victim's room. He continued, "Now, excuse me, I must investigate—the Duke's Rangers must be told of this tragedy. Stand aside, let me pass."

Ember gave ground with poor grace, allowing the taverner into the murder room. The gnome from the end of the hallway moved up to Hennet and handed him some leather leggings and boots. Hennet dressed himself without embarrassment in the hallway. Ember paid no attention; she watched the taverner. All that nose-rubbing and sweating . . . the man was hiding something.

The taverner walked without much confidence into the room, gazed on the sight, and gagged. When he turned away, his eyes were glazed. He was whispering to himself, apparently forgetting Ember's presence at the door.

"I've got to get them out of here. Out! No amount of money is worth more of this."

With a wheeze and a gasp, he rushed back into the hallway and thundered down the stairs two at a time.

Ember glanced at Hennet, who was fully dressed, and said, "The taverner—he knows what happened." Without another word, she glided down the stairs after him. The man and the gnome followed her.

The stairs emptied into the common room on the main floor. It held neither Brek Gorunn nor the taverner. Ember heard a clatter in the kitchen. She darted through the half-doors separating the two rooms. Fire danced in a fireplace, and herbs and meats hung from the ceiling. A scattering of iron pots and pans lay on the floor near a wooden rack on the wall. Otherwise the kitchen was orderly and empty.

Hennet and the gnome followed her in, both breathing hard.

"Wait, we want to help!" said Hennet. The gnome looked surprised but said nothing.

Ember paused, then replied, "Fine. What do you suggest?"

The gnome lowered a pair of goggles over his eyes and said, "I'm Nebin Raulnor, a wizard of the arcane arts. Last night I saw something odd in the hallway. I thought it was a dream." The gnome ducked his head, as if ashamed.

Hennet clapped

The gnome on the shoulder. "Are you saying you went out into the hallway last night and saw something there? Why didn't you wake me?" As he spoke, Hennet studied the kitchen. "Those fallen pots seem strangely untidy, compared to the rest of the place."

Ember rushed to the utensil rack from which the pots had fallen. The wall seemed slightly off kilter, as if its foundation was sinking unevenly—or as if the wall had been moved slightly from its proper place. She put a hand against the iron rack and pushed. With a click, the wall swung way, obviously on a hinge. Beyond was a lightless stairwell leading downward.

Hennet looked into the darkness and said, "How did you know the wall was false?"

"Lucky."

Nebin approached more slowly, looking down the stairs. "You want to go down there?" he asked, looking at Ember, then Hennet.

In answer, Hennet spoke a few words of magic, and his index finger burst into light, bright as a torch, though it gave no heat.

"Show off," sniffed Nebin.

Ember took the lead, followed by Hennet, then the gnome. The stairs were old and worn smooth. Dust was heaped along every margin and corner. Hennet's enchanted light showed a clear path of footprints through the dust.

He whispered, "More than one person has gone this way."

The steps led down to a closed door. A seam of light spilled from beneath it, brighter than Hennet's light. Ember heard murmuring voices. She motioned for silence and sidled up to the door, putting her ear to it. Two voices spoke. One was the taverner, sounding scared. The other voice didn't speak, it just grunted, yet it seemed somehow familiar, which disturbed Ember. In the background, she heard a snatch of prayer—Brek Gorunn?

Ember slammed the door open. Beyond was an earthen chamber supported by stone columns, hung round with greenish lamps. The taverner spoke to two men in red masks! The masks were pulled down around their necks so that their faces were visible. Behind them, a red-masked woman bent over the dwarf, Brek. He sat stiffly with his back to a stone column. His beefy hands were lashed behind him and around the pillar.

"Face me, Nerull-worshipers!" yelled Ember.

She launched a flying kick at the taverner's back. Her foot connected, sending the heavy-set man sprawling into the shadows.

All were caught off guard, including Hennet and Nebin, who stood dumbfounded on the stairs. Neither of them had seen or even heard of these red-masked strangers before, obviously, or heard the name of Nerull spoken in anything but a child's rhyme. It was painfully obvious, however, that the people in the room were up to no good, if the trussed-up dwarf was any indication.

One of the kidnappers regained his composure ahead of the rest. He sprang to attack Ember, using his hands and feet as weapons. Again Ember wondered what deranged order these red-masked devils represented. The man leered at her, his mouth gaping—it was her tongueless former captive! His broken arm and all of his other, lesser injuries were healed, clearly the work of magic. As recognition flashed on Ember's face, her opponent barked out a grating, self-satisfied laugh.

The other red-masked man, more portly and slower than the first, stood back and began chanting. A sickle hung at his side, stained and rusted from much use and little upkeep. On his finger flashed a ring inscribed with the symbol of the skull and sickle. He was a priest of Nerull!

The woman near Brek Gorunn straightened and grabbed a light crossbow slung from her side. It was already cocked. She tried to draw a bead on Ember, but couldn't get a clear shot. She shifted her aim to Hennet, who still stood in the doorway.

Hennet was not unprepared. As the crossbow came up, he released two bolts of his own from his already glowing finger-tip. The sorcerous missiles of enchanted force unerringly slammed into the woman. She gasped, but remained upright and fired her crossbow back at the sorcerer. The bolt, retracing the path of Hennet's magical strike, caught the sorcerer in his left arm.

He grunted in pain and surprise. Nebin stepped up next to his wounded friend. The gnome still wore his goggles over his eyes, and in his hands he grasped a wand. It was carved of alder and tipped with a tiny, shining stone. The gnome sighted along the wand, and a splash of clashing colors sprang from the tip to strike the woman trying to re-cock her crossbow. She yelped and dropped to the floor, senseless.

Nebin crowed, "I got one!"

Ember's foe was more cautious than when he last faced her in Volanth. This time he held back, fighting defensively. Three kicks were deflected, and four brutal open-hand blows came to nothing. The man danced to the side, ducked, and backed away, taking little real hurt from her onslaught, but he refrained from exposing himself with attacks of his own. Ember had little time to wonder what he was waiting for.

The portly man's chanting ceased; the priest of Nerull had finished his invocation. A spark of pale green light appeared in midair. The spark gained volume and shape over the space of a heartbeat, and a horror materialized from the sickening light.

The beast was shaped something like a newborn human child, crossed with a giant slug. It was almost man-sized, but it oozed along the floor like a worm, dripping with pale green slime. Its visage was pure horror. The gnome quivered for a moment, then turned and ran.

Ember felt a wave of fear break over her. Her insides churned as her throat constricted to a knot. She wanted to scream, to faint, but most of all to flee. She shot a desperate look at Hennet. The sorcerer seemed to be wavering on the doorstep. Terror twisted his face into a grotesque mask, yet the look from Ember galvanized him.

He yelled, "Nebin! Get back here!"

But the gnome's footfalls were already fading up the stairwell. Ember was glad for any company at all.

The priest of Nerull called aloud to the slug-thing, "Serve us, as we have served you, oh Abyssal Child, oh Servitor of our lord Nerull." He clutched his sickle and moved toward Ember.

The horrid child-face of the slug regarded Hennet. Then it spoke in its cracked, pipe-organ voice, declaring, "I'm going to eat you. First your hands, then your feet, then your heart."

The sorcerer recoiled in disgust. As the abyssal child squirmed toward him, Hennet made a great leap over the thing's back. The creature snapped at him but missed. Ember breathed easier when she saw the sorcerer dart up to Brek Gorunn's side.

If I don't do something to even the odds, thought Ember, these two will finish me.

As the priest's scythe arced toward her, she moved as if to step backward. Lured on by the ruse, the priest stepped forward only to meet the full impact of Ember's circle kick to the crown of his head. She felt the blow travel up her arch into the muscles of her leg. It was a good strike, and the priest fell like a stone.

The abyssal child wormed toward Hennet, who sawed frantically at Brek Gorunn's bindings with a dagger.

"Come on, man!" yelped the dwarf, with his eye on the monster.

Not a second too soon, the line parted. Hennet fell back and the dwarf leaped up and to the side, toward the corner where his captors had tossed his warhammer.

Whirling and striking at the same time, the dwarf swung his hammer desperately and bounced it across the creature's rounded back. Even that glancing blow brought a scream from the monstrous thing, followed by a gobbet of acid. The liquid struck Brek's mail armor, where it sizzled and fumed into a thin line of curling smoke.

Hennet murmured another spell to release two more magical bolts of enchantment. They whined through the air and scorched into the creature, which was barely beyond the sorcerer's reach. It quivered, expanded, and spewed a noxious cloud that fouled the air in the small room as it collapsed. A second later, it faded away as if it had never been.

Brek Gorunn rushed up behind Ember's opponent. Caught off guard, the red-masked man tried to run, but the dwarf's deadly hammer sent him crashing to the stone floor.

Ember, Brek Gorunn, Hennet the sorcerer, and the gnome Nebin sat together in the common room of the tavern. They talked quietly of the morning's events.

Two Nerullan cultists were dead and would cause no more trouble. It was clear, however, that after years of banishment, the cult of Nerull was becoming active once again. The taverner may have been merely a dupe, paid for the use of his root cellar and his silence. The murdered woman's companions promised to take him back to Volanth, the closest institution of law. The red-masked cultists were a different matter.

Ember said, "It is a strange coincidence to find the cult here at this inn, unless its influence is wider than I thought. Brek Gorunn and I are on our way to New Koratia to warn my order about the cult's strange hatred of the Enabled Hand."

"'Strange hatred?'" asked Hennet.

"Her chapter in Volanth was wiped out," supplied Brek Gorunn. "We're pretty sure that was done by Nerullan cultists, too."

Nebin gulped, and Hennet said, "I'm so sorry! I. . . ."

"Thank you," replied Ember, expressionless.

"Guess what, Hennet and I are on our way to New Koratia, too," said the gnome. "We're competing in the Duel Arcane. Why don't we go together? They say companions on the road make long journeys shorter. Besides, Hennet has heard all my stories too many times—I need a fresh audience." The gnome laughed.

"What a good idea, Nebin!" enthused Hennet, sitting forward. He stole a quick glance at the monk. "Well, that is, if you'll have us?"

Brek grunted. "A fine idea. Security on the road and all that. Ember?"

"It could be dangerous. If you're willing to join forces, you're more than welcome," said Ember. "You had no cause to help us, but you did anyway. If I could reward you, I would. Accept my thanks instead."

"Anyone would have done the same," said Hennet.

"No one else did."

The travelers gathered their gear and met in the courtyard. The two spellcasters were traveling by horse-drawn wagon. Ember and Brek Gorunn had walked from Volanth, and were happy to continue their journey by wagon instead of on foot.

As Hennet led the horses from the inn's stable, he said, "This is Rain, the other Dust. I bought them two weeks ago, and they have served us well."

He hitched the horses, and motioned the others to board. The wagon was a simple coach, with two bench seats and some room for baggage beneath the seats. It was in serviceable condition, though it wasn't covered; passengers would be alternately baked by the sun and drenched by the rain, if it came to that. Still, Ember

quickly decided that it was a wonderful contrivance for long journeys. Before long the group was trotting down the road at a steady
pace, Hennet driving in the front seat with the reigns clutched
in both hands.

The road was in remarkable repair, allowing the travelers to
laugh off the worst of the bumps. Often, the road ran straight and
wide through low, level grasslands. Other times it wound through
deep groves of conifer trees. Farms and small communities were
closely spaced along the road. Once, as they rolled easily over a
commanding rise, Ember could see ahead to the gently rising and
falling grassland dotted with clumps of trees, all gently melting
away into a green, grassy haze in the distance. The road ran
straight on until it too disappeared in the faraway blur.

"Am I crazed?" wondered Brek Gorunn.

Hennet had passed him the reigns earlier at his request. He
knew far less about driving horses than the sorcerer, but
wanted to give it a try.

"Relax!" laughed Hennet, who stood behind him. "The
horses can sense your tension. Really, you don't need to pull on
the reigns so much. The horses know what to do. Only use the
reigns in an emergency."

The dwarf sucked in a big breath and slowly let it out. Sure
enough, once he relaxed and loosened his grip on the reigns, the
going seemed easier. The horses plodded along, oblivious to his
crisis of doubt. He allowed himself a small grin under his beard.

"Perhaps I am getting the hang of this."

Hennet watched the dwarf linger for a short time. As each
minute passed, Brek's confidence swelled.

He said, "Go on, sit down, I've got it licked."

Hennet nodded and turned to find his seat among the other
passengers. Ember sat on a wagon bench, facing sideways, one
hand propping up her head. Nebin's nose was in his book of spells

and his mouth was muttering. Glancing back occasionally, Brek could see that the sorcerer wanted to speak with Ember, but seemed uncertain.

Hennet finally sat down next to Ember. The sorcerer touched Ember's shoulder and asked if she was comfortable. The dwarf couldn't help overhearing when the two began talking—they were all sitting in the same wagon.

Ember sighed. She looked out past the slowly scrolling landscape for a second before saying, "Sometimes I lose myself in the moment. I find myself enjoying the scenery, or absorbed in an exercise of my order. I look up and see a cloud that reminds me of something and for a moment I forget the reason for my trip. But when that happens, something else inside me says, 'you can't be happy.' Then I remember what happened to my chapter in Volanth. It comes back to me.

"They were all my friends."

She lapsed into silence, and Hennet was silent for a few seconds, as well. Brek glanced back and saw that the sorcerer was fumbling with his cloak.

Finally, Hennet said, "I'm sure I don't know what you're going through. But, I know that with enough time, things improve. It's getting through until then—that's the trick."

"Easy to say, hard to bear," said Ember.

Hennet remained quiet this time. Brek Gorunn mused on what he knew of his companions. The dwarf had known Ember for only the short time he'd worked with the Volanth chapter. She was the stalwart sort, for a human. She had suffered a grievous blow, but showed every sign of pulling through.

He wondered about the sorcerer. The dwarf expected that Hennet meant well. That was the human way, to "talk things out." Not like dwarves. They drew their strength from personal detachment and from turning inward when things went sour.

The travelers made good time. The weather remained fine, clear, and cool. With the aid of the wagon, several days of relatively pleasant travel passed. At night they camped along the roadside, drawing up sometimes near other weary travelers. For the most part, they passed only farmers on the road, moving locally between the small villages to sell their produce. They also passed a caravan traveling the opposite direction, a group of sellswords down on their luck, and a company of Peloran brothers, marching across the country, nearly blind from too many adoring glances into the fiery sun.

In this way, the group finally came to the city of New Koratia.

New Koratia was built at the intersection of the Duke's Road and mighty River Delnir. Four centuries earlier, the Baron Dammeral, eager for his own lands, broke away from the Kingdom of Soes and founded Koratia as the seat of his government. Dammeral, his government, and even the Kingdom of Soes were long gone, but the duchy of Koratia remained. The city was an important trade hub, ideally situated on those two great thoroughfares. Fortunes were made in lost in New Koratia, but the city continued to grow.

Hennet drove the wagon up to the open city gates. Burly guards paid them little attention as their rough coach rolled under the stone arch and into town. A wide avenue opened up before them. On it, they merged into the throng of others entering the city, moving down the crowded, sun-warmed avenue.

Tall buildings, three and four stories in height, framed the main road on either side. Smaller streets leading off the main thoroughfare quickly twisted away into tenement-lined alleys, courtyards filled with tents, bazaars, and shops, only to spill out unexpectedly onto another large road. A thousand exotic smells wafted through the air, and the languages of many people and races mingled into a single buzz. To the east, the buildings gave way to warehouses and then to docks, where the river merchants bought and sold their wares. Many things could be had in New Koratia, some truly marvelous and exotic. The city's market district was the wonder of the region.

Farther along the main avenue, gilded towers rose to majestic heights. The duchy's nobles lived there. The towers were striking to behold as they sparkled in the sun, but even these paled when compared to the glistening cylinder of glass that floated without visible support above the city's center. It was carved with many balconies and stairways, and its tip shone brilliantly with a light all its own. Low-drifting clouds sometimes got entangled among the highest balconies, the people of New Koratia liked to tell strangers.

"Though I've never before seen it, I've heard it described; that is the Floating Crystal, home to the famed College of Wizardry," said Hennet. "They sponsor the Duel Arcane every three years."

The gnome nodded, and added, "I bet the city's thick with our ilk, Hennet. They've come from all over to compete. I can smell the magic." He gave a demonstrative sniff, then winked.

Ember said, "It's time I sought the Order of the Enabled Hand. My warning can't wait."

"And we must hasten to the Floating Crystal. We need to sign up for the duel straight away," replied Nebin.

Hennet looked a little sad as he helped Ember and Brek Gorunn pack up their belongings from the wagon. He said, "Though we've traveled together only a few days, you are both friends to me." Hennet glanced at Ember as he said the last, then looked quickly away.

"My friendship was won when you rescued me from the cellar," replied Brek. "I give you Moradin's blessing and our thanks. We'll meet again, I'm certain."

Ember nodded, half listening to the dwarf but obviously impatient to be about her business.

Hennet spoke in a rush. "Let's not leave it up to chance. Perhaps we can meet later this week? Nebin and I will be competing in the duel; perhaps you can come see us? We're staying at the Cuttlestone, a tavern just up the street from here."

He motioned to a nearby signboard, on which vacant rooms were advertised at several inns, including the Cuttlestone.

"I do not know what the Order will ask of me," said Ember. "Better we make no plans now, lest we be forced to break them later. What will be, will be. Good luck in the duel."

She patted Hennet on the shoulder. With that, the monk and the dwarf turned and walked into the mass of people on the great avenue. Soon, they were lost from sight.

Nebin nudged his friend, as Hennet watched them go. "We'll see them again," he chided. "Come on, or we'll be late."

Hennet sighed, returned to his seat, and headed the wagon down the crowded streets of New Koratia.

The sorcerer and the diminutive wizard found a clean-enough barn in New Koratia where they could stable their horses. The rent for keeping their wagon was more than they were willing to pay; Hennet solved the problem by selling it to the stable-master. With the extra money, they could afford better lodging at the Cuttlestone.

Hennet and Nebin pushed through the crush of people heading toward the Floating Crystal. Without such an obvious landmark, they'd have been hard pressed to find the location of the Duel Arcane. Soon enough they stood at the edge of a large, open space beneath the hovering tower. Nebin could feel the tower's presence above even while not looking. Despite his wizardly training, his unconscious mind had decided that the building was about to crash down. He didn't share this feeling with Hennet, who seemed oblivious to the hanging threat.

The clear space was a coliseum. It was open on one end, but the other half was built up in great stone seats, like a half-bowl. The coliseum's floor was divided into more than a dozen circular areas. Scores of people, most of them in robes, some in outlandish costumes, including one woman with a brilliantly glowing glass cape, congregated across the floor of the coliseum. Some circles contained people who chanted, waved their hands, and occasionally released displays of magical energy.

"The preliminaries have already started!" said Hennet.

The two hurried down to an official-looking elf in bright green robes. The elf, like a few others, had the emblem of a floating tower on his robe. He looked up.

"We're here to compete in the Duel Arcane, if we are not too late," said Hennet.

The elf raised an elegant eyebrow, then grinned.

"You fear that you have missed the deadline, yes? Not to worry. Preliminaries conclude today. Are you entering the competition for the Golden Wand? Neither of you is secretly an arcane master masquerading as a novice caster?" He produced a monocle from a silk pouch, brought it to his eye, and squinted at them through it. "No, I would know. Very well, that's your group."

The elf pointed toward a gathering near the middle of the coliseum, and Hennet and Nebin wound their way out onto the floor, following the official's directions. The seats of the coliseum were mostly empty. The preliminaries were not nearly as exciting as the main events of the Duel Arcane. The people in the stands at this early stage would be mostly professional gamblers and bookmakers, trying to pick up every tidbit of information they could on possible winners. Nebin had been told that the main event drew over ten thousand spectators. His stomach fluttered at the thought.

They reached their group, which included an elf woman in a blue tunic holding a wand, a halfling man with a dwarf-like beard, and three humans.

Another official wearing the badge of the floating tower

pointed to the elf woman and said, "Follow me, please."

She paled, but obliged, and was led toward one of the circles.

One of the humans turned and grinned at Nebin. "She shouldn't be so nervous," he said. "These are the preliminaries. All we need to do is show magical proficiency."

The man pointed at a pebble lying near his feet. A ghostly hand appeared, picked up the pebble, and dropped it in one of Nebin's pockets.

The man laughed and added. "I'm sure we're all up to that. By the way, my name is Aganon. Aganon Redstone."

Nebin warmed to the man, who appeared both so friendly and so confident at the same time. A bit like himself, he fancied.

"I am Nebin Raulnor, adept of the Secret Flame."

"Secret Flame, eh? I haven't heard of that enchantment."

Nebin grinned. "Then, watch and learn, my friend!"

The gnome lowered his goggles, then loosed the same spell he had used several days earlier at the Inn of the Fair Warrior. It rarely failed to impress. As before, he created the image of a ball of raging fire. This time, he placed the ball several feet above his head. Phantom sparks rained down, partially cloaking him in fauxfire. He spread his arms wide to promote his own spectacle.

"Ah, see, the Secret Flame responds to my every whim!"

Those standing in the group with Nebin, Aganon, and Hennet studied the floating flame, but quickly turned back to study the field—it was hard to impress a wizard with a wizard's trick. To Nebin's satisfaction, Aganon took a step back as if impressed.

"Gnome, I have met my better! Truly, you must be a powerful wizard if you can so easily command so potent a force," said Aganon, concluding his speech with a slight bow.

Nebin was pleased but suspicious. He could never be certain

when humans were being sarcastic; sarcasm was rare in gnomish culture. Before Nebin could offer a rejoinder, someone tapped him on the shoulder.

A Duel Arcane official stood behind Nebin, an open scroll penned with many rules in hand. Nebin let the illusion of the fire fade and pushed his goggles up onto his head.

"Yes? I'm Nebin Raulnor. Am I up?"

The official frowned and said, "The rules of the duel forbid non-competitive casting in the coliseum. It could interfere with the legitimate judging of other competitors. Please explain why I shouldn't disqualify you right now?"

Nebin hesitated, scrabbling for an explanation.

Melf's Beard, he thought frantically, I'm going to disqualify myself before I even qualify.

Aganon stepped up. "My new acquaintance was showing me the crucial finale to a heroic story," he said. "I'm afraid the story wouldn't have been the same without the visual aid. Surely you won't ruin such a wonderful tale by ejecting its teller, especially when he's so talented a wizard."

The official, apparently interested despite himself, asked, "What story?"

Aganon looked to the gnome.

Nebin stuttered, "Well, you see, I . . . I was on the road to attend this very competition. Then . . . then . . ." Suddenly he smiled. "On the way to the magnificent city, I and my companions stayed at an inn, one with a reputation for being haunted by ghosts. I was out late at night searching for magical essences of moon dust—you can't collect them by day, you know—when I heard a call for help. I responded instantly, and found a fellow traveler being menaced by a horrible creature slithering about on its belly! If I hadn't shown up, I shudder to think what would have happened. I used the very spell I just displayed to send that terrible creature running. The poor woman was so grateful. She told me that if ever the Order of the Enabled Hand could do me a favor, I shouldn't hesitate to ask."

Nebin smiled as he finished the story.

The official studied the gnome, scratched his chin, and said, "I'm feeling generous. I won't disqualify you. But another infraction, and you're out."

He moved off, shaking his head, and Nebin let out a long breath.

"Who knew they were such sticklers? Aganon, I owe you a drink."

The human nodded, but he was looking quizzically at the gnome. He seemed about to say something, but instead darted a look between Nebin and Hennet, who was being led out to one of the circular areas by an official, and he smiled enigmatically.

"I'd like that, Nebin," he replied. "Where can I find you and your friend—what did you say his name is?"

"Hennet. He likes to believe his mastery of the craft is as potent as my own. Out of friendship, I indulge him. We're staying at a little inn off Cuttlestone Row—the Cuttlestone Inn. Look us up."

Aganon answered, "I will. I would love to hear more about this terrible beast and the poor Enabled Hand monk."

Another official motioned at Aganon. It was time for his proficiency test.

Nebin frowned. He wondered if he should have been so free with his identity and purposes with a stranger.

Well, I'm sure it's all right, rationalized the gnome. Aganon is certainly friendly, he thought.

With that, he pushed the doubt from his mind and turned it to preparing for his test.

The Motherhouse of the Enabled Hand was as grand as Ember remembered. An edifice of whitewashed stone, the structure was ringed around with elegant and overpowering relief sculpture. The frieze portrayed an ongoing fight of monk versus monk and stretched all the way around the building, creating an unbroken loop. The monks of the Hand were a legendary force, and few other groups in the duchy could claim such a prestigious and powerful membership, nor such a stately and arresting home.

Ember and Brek Gorunn walked down a long flagstone path through the colorful garden that surrounded the Motherhouse. The scent of rose mixed with sage and pine made her think of her youth. Together with the bountiful flowers and stately white building, the Motherhouse presented an air of serene strength. Ember felt sure that things would soon be made right. She especially looked forward to meeting her old mentor, Kairoth.

The wide door of the Motherhouse was open. Immediately inside was a large chamber, a salon draped with colorful linens and flagged with granite tile. Three novitiate monks sat, in apparent mediation, facing the doorway. As Ember and Brek Gorunn walked up, the foremost stood and bowed.

"Greetings. Welcome to the Order of the Enabled Hand." Recognizing Ember's dress, she ventured a ritual greeting of the order, "Weakness is pain."

Ember bowed. "But pain leaves the body."

The novitiate concluded, "And so weakness is purged. Welcome! From what chapter do you hail, sister?"

Ember said, "Until recently, Volanth Chapter. But that chapter is no more."

The novitiate paused, not understanding.

Ember said, "Sister, I must see one of the elders immediately. I bring dire news that may endanger the whole order."

The novitiate who had spoken looked back to the other young

trainees who remained seated, a man and another woman. They had no answers for her except concerned expressions. The novitiate turned back to Ember and Brek Gorunn.

"Wait here. I will ask leave to disturb the elders in their inner *dojo*."

With that, she glided away.

Apparently things had changed a bit since Ember's days as a novice. When she trained, things were slightly less formal. She shrugged it off and looked at one of the remaining novitiates.

"Is this the first you have heard of troubles for the order in Volanth?"

One of the remaining two novitiates stood up. He wore the same simple white practice garment as the other trainees.

He swallowed and said, "No, nothing definite, but there were rumors."

The other trainee coughed and shook her head slightly.

The novitiate continued, "We were told that the rumors were groundless, and that we shouldn't repeat lies."

He looked into Ember's eyes, as if trying to read her intentions.

Ember nearly flushed. "Lies they are not. Volanth chapter is destroyed, and enemies of the Enabled Hand are abroad. You can repeat that all you like, because I speak only truth."

The novitiate backed up a step and muttered an apology under his breath. He looked down and refused to meet the gaze of Ember or the dwarf.

After that, the minutes passed uncomfortably. The trainees said no more, and neither did Ember. She heard Brek Gorunn mutter a prayer under his breath, asking Moradin to bequeath the blessing of tolerance.

Finally the original novitiate returned. She said, "Sister, please proceed directly to the inner *dojo*, the Elders' Sanctum. Two await you, Elder Cestra and Elder Vobod."

The novitiate motioned back in the direction she had come.

Ember led her friend the dwarf down the hallway without a backward glance. She was still a bit angry, but knew it was not part of the Order's code to display negative emotions. She was slightly ashamed to have been so obvious in front of novitiates.

They passed several open courtyards where monks of various degrees trained. The sounds of their exercise soothed her. She and Brek moved down a long corridor lit with lamps on either side and numerous small, closed doors. Ember remembered spending many a long day in those rooms; meditation cubicles, where a student attempted to quiet the mind and enhance inner strength. As they approached the Elders' Sanctum, she wondered about her old mentor Kairoth and why he wasn't with the other elders. In fact, it was odd that the usual quorum of five elders were not assembled in the inner *dojo*.

They passed a richly carved oaken lintel and entered the inner *dojo*. Silk screens hid the walls, though warm lights and fragrant oils burned behind them, giving the space a special ambience. Three people stood within, their hands clasped in the posture of respectful waiting. Ember wondered what activity she had interrupted with her arrival. One of the three monks wore the sash of a teacher, not an elder. Though his face was as stony as the two elders, Ember thought she detected deference in his posture, as he stood a little apart and behind the elders.

Elder Vobod stepped forward. Ember remembered him from long ago, but only barely. His head was shaved, except for a braid of gray hair that hung down his back, though his eyebrows and thin mustache were dark. His green silk robe was elegant, embroidered with many flecks of gemstone. On his finger flashed a large ring inset with a strange symbol unfamiliar to Ember.

"Be welcome in the hands of the Enabled." He motioned to the instructor, who closed the door behind Ember and Brek Gorunn.

Elder Vobod smiled thinly, saying, "We prefer to keep this interview private. We know of your plight—"

Despite the breach in protocol, Ember broke in, "You know that Volanth chapter was beset and destroyed by enemies of the Hand? Not according to the novitiates minding the door."

The other elder, a human female whom Ember recognized as Elder Cestra, raised a hand and said, "Your questions have answers. Sit, calm yourself. Your words betray your emotions. The Order has taught you better."

Cestra's hair was dark, long, and gathered into a braid much longer than Vobod's. Her eyes were dark and penetrating. Her silk robe, while elegant, was less showy than Vobod's. Ember remembered her in a kindly way, though she'd had little contact with the elder during her training.

Censured, Ember sat and said no more. She motioned for Brek Gorunn to join her.

The dwarf continued to stand, saying, "Dwarves are not suited to such contortions. I will stand, if you don't mind."

Apparently, the elders did not mind; they ignored the dwarf.

Elder Vobod looked at Ember and said, "Sister Ember, we know about the tragedy in Volanth, and you have our condolences. We share your grief."

Ember looked back at him, puzzled.

Elder Cestra said, "Sister Ember, though your journey of warning is commendable, know that we in the Motherhouse are aware of our enemies. They revealed themselves prior to the attack in Volanth. We blame ourselves for underestimating the danger these villains posed. We assumed the threat was local to the Motherhouse. Had we known that our outlying chapter houses were threatened, we would have sent word to the elders of each. We have done so now."

Ember ventured, "Why do the novices at the door speak

in ignorance, knowing only rumors and lies?"

Vobod spoke. "Though the threat seems extreme, we have determined that the novitiates and those below the rank of instructor should remain ignorant, lest they be moved to fear or unwise acts that would compromise our own investigation."

"Sister Ember," said Cestra, "even now, most of the surviving elders are looking into this matter, attempting to root out those who would do us harm. So, too, are our most trusted instructors. We anticipate soon putting this terrible event behind us."

Ember said, "I don't think you understand the magnitude of the threat that faces us. Volanth chapter was wiped out to the last! I am the only survivor. See? I wear Loku's Bracers, relics of the founder of our chapter. There is no other to wear them now. But there is more; on the road between Volanth, we were assaulted by a new nest of these Nerull cultists. They seem to be everywhere!"

Elder Cestra paused, looked at Vobod, and said, "Nerull cultists? Is this something new?"

Vobod nodded quickly, saying, "Yes, yes, we knew this. Some who oppose us give allegiance to that old god. Forgive me Cestra, if I do not keep you appraised of every latest development. It is a minor detail. More important are the events of this morning: We discovered and destroyed their last stronghold here in New Koratia."

Ember gasped. "Their last? But why did some old cult wish us harm in the first place? What are we to them?"

Cestra turned back to Ember and said, "Elder Vobod is in charge of the Enabled Hand's response to the threat. He leads with the other elders in this matter. I was chosen as the lone elder to keep the Motherhouse running in the meantime." She smiled, turning to face Vobod again. "But, Elder Vobod, please speak on. Sister Ember has endured much and deserves to know the whole story."

"Very well," Vobod responded. "Apparently a cleric of Nerull called Sosfane was behind the plot to destroy the Enabled Hand. Sosfane led a group of disaffected monks from the south, who are known to walk paths of evil. But Sosfane was slain in her putrid lair below New Koratia this very morning, as well as all those who followed her. I am only now waiting for confirmation from Elder Breshimon, who leads in the field. With Sosfane dead, our order is once again assured of peace. It was she who masterminded the entire threat. It only remains to mop up scattered bits and pieces of the enemy and conclude the investigation."

Cestra, looking from Vobod to Ember, said, "So now you know. Everything will soon be right again."

Ember felt dumbfounded. After all she had seen and the days she spent on the road to bring warning to the Enabled Hand, she was finding it difficult to accept that everything had already been taken care of.

She said, "Elders, surely there is more to this—what did this Sosfane have against us? Was she crazed, or was she acting for some deeper purpose?"

Vobod shook his head. "Who can say why? She is dead now, so we cannot know the truth from her lips. Our investigation will, of course, reveal her motivation in time. Please allow me to contribute in some way to the final eradication of these monsters."

"I'm afraid there is nothing for you to do. We understand your desire to be useful in this effort, but we cannot manufacture a threat from nothing. The matter is already resolved."

Cestra offered, "You are welcome to stay on the grounds as long as you like. When your grief is assuaged, you can remain here at the Motherhouse if you like. Perhaps you would care to teach for a while? We always welcome *sa bum nim*."

Ember wiped her forehead and said, "No, thank you Elder Cestra. At least, let me think on it. Really, all I want is to talk to my old friend Kairoth. Elder Kairoth, I mean. Is he involved in the effort against the cultists?"

Elder Cestra looked distressed.

Elder Vobod sighed and said, "I'm sorry, Ember. Kairoth was one of the first slain by the enemy. It was his sacrifice that alerted us to the enemy's true nature. It was a terrible loss for all of us; we still grieve."

"Slain? But when?"

"He was taken from us some four weeks past. Elder Vobod, here, found his body," said Cestra.

Vobod nodded. "A harder blow I've never felt. Kairoth was one of my dearest friends. And it was on the Day of Fasting, too, Kairoth's favorite yearly festival. He will be remembered always," vowed the elder.

"But . . ." stammered Ember. Something was wrong. Her last letter from Kairoth was clearly dated three days after the Day of Fasting. Ember nearly flushed—she almost betrayed her reaction.

She nearly called Elder Vobod a liar.

In the end, she held her tongue. Something was very, very wrong. Until she knew who to trust, Ember decided it would be best to remain silent.

A sharp rap on the door roused Hennet from meditation. He looked at Nebin, who was deep in a dusty tome, penning notes in the margin with an inked quill. The gnome had purchased the volume on their way back from the Duel Arcane preliminaries. Both he and Nebin had qualified, despite Nebin nearly disqualifying himself. After the preliminaries, he and the gnome secured lodging at the Cuttlestone Inn.

Hennet sighed; Nebin wasn't going to get the door. The sorcerer stood, arranged his cape, and answered. It was Ember and the dwarf, Brek Gorunn.

Is she here to see me? wondered Hennet.

He stood unspeaking for a moment, tongue-tied, before he managed to say, "Come in. How did your visit to the Motherhouse go?"

"Seemed to go well," Said Brek Gorunn. The dwarf looked at the monk. "To me, at least."

He had the air of someone who knew more than he said.

Ember entered and clasped hands with Hennet, then said, "I apologize for interrupting your afternoon, but besides Brek Gorunn I don't know anyone else I can trust in New Koratia, except for you two."

Nebin closed his book at this declaration, curious to hear more.

"Us two?" repeated Hennet. "What about the Motherhouse? Surely the Enabled Hand is trustworthy."

"Something strange is going on there. With your indulgence, I'd like to tell you."

Hennet said, "Of course!"

He saw the gnome hide a smirk behind his book, but he didn't care. If Ember wanted to tell him a story, he wouldn't deny her.

Ember spoke, telling of the visit to the Motherhouse. She related how the elders assured her that the threat to the order was eliminated, though she could scarcely credit the news. She further explained how her old friend, Kairoth, was lost to that same threat, on the Day of Fasting.

"So," continued Ember, "I have a difficult time explaining this. I didn't show the letter to the elders, or even mention it; caution warned me against revealing my knowledge."

Everyone clustered close around Ember as she opened her

satchel and extracted a leather parchment sleeve, of the variety used by couriers to send messages overland.

She said, "I received this letter from Kairoth after the Day of Fasting. And look—" She pointed to the wax seal on the leather sleeve. The seal was broken, but the date pressed into the wax could still be read. "See the date? This letter was sent three days after the Day of Fasting, but according to Elder Vobod, he found Kairoth's body on the Day of Fasting. Kairoth isn't dead, or wasn't, yet the elders lied about it."

Hennet felt a surge of excitement over the mystery and treachery revealed by the date on the letter. He loved puzzles; of course, never before had he dealt with a puzzle that involved murder.

"If they lied about this, what else did they lie to me about?" concluded Ember.

Nebin shrugged and said, "You know your own order better than we. Perhaps a simple mistake is to blame?"

Hennet, seeing Nebin's tack, said, "Or perhaps the message is incorrectly dated?"

Brek Gorunn cleared his throat, then said, "Could it be that, denied your vengeance against those who destroyed Volanth chapter, your mind seeks enemies in the shadows where there are none?"

"I would like to believe any of those explanations," replied Ember, "but it is not in the nature of an Enabled Hand elder to mistake the date of the death of a member, or for an elder to mistakenly date a letter. Something rings false."

So saying, she removed a single piece of parchment from the leather sleeve. Neat script covered the parchment, apparently the last message of Elder Kairoth.

"But, it does no good," she continued. "He mentions no enemies of the Order, Nerull, or anything out of the ordinary."

Hennet reached for the letter and aksed, "May I?"

Ember handed the letter to him. Hennet read it aloud.

Sister Ember,

It has been too long since you last visited the Motherhouse. The gardens are in full summer bloom. The Day of Fasting is three days past, and we missed your presence. Sometimes the smell of the flowers is so strong it puts me in mind of the old days. Remember when we explored below the city, looking for that old temple? We spent three (3) whole days down there; I wonder if you remember? Well, it hardly matters, I suppose. Things go on much as they ever have. The Motherhouse is training a new crop of novitiates, though I fear some of the class are less then apt to the lessons of the order.

Most sincerely,
Kairoth of the Enabled Hand

Hennet read the letter through twice. Random letters were smudged along the bottom of the paper, apparently thoughtlessly scribbled letters as one might make when distracted, but still holding the quill. They seemed out of keeping with the neat script of the rest of the letter.

He pointed them out to Ember and asked, "Do these mean anything to you?"

"Merely doodles, I think," she said. She ran a hand through her cropped, curled hair. Hennet wished it was his hand, and the thought so distracted him that he almost missed what she said next. "But something else is odd. I didn't give this letter a second thought, because I wasn't looking for anything strange. On second glance, it seems odd for Kairoth to mention that old adventure. We have talked of it often enough, but it was long ago. It's an old story, and out of context. We spent less than a day looking for the temple below the city, as well he knows. Certainly nothing like three days."

Nebin volunteered, "Is he getting old and forgetful?"

Ember replied, "No, his mind is as sharp as ever. I can't imagine why he would make such a special point of incorrectly recalling the number of days."

"Maybe three is somehow important?" ventured Hennet.

Nebin, who was sitting at the table, said abruptly, "Maybe it's part of a cipher. Gnomes often use ciphers. Some of the oldest writings inscribed by our ancestors are in the form of ciphers. That's how they're kept safe from being read by the wrong people. Without the key, they're incomprehensible."

"The key?" asked Brek Gorunn, uncertain about the gnome's tack. "Wouldn't a simple spell do the trick?"

"No," answered the gnome. "Magic can be broken by magic, revealing the hidden message even it it's in a language the reader doesn't understand. But if a mundane cipher is used to encode a deeper meaning within the letters, there is no magic to dispel. The letters are merely letters. They have a double meaning only for the person who knows the key."

The gnome reached for the letter, which Hennet surrendered.

"Now, even the simplest cipher must have a key," continued Nebin, pontificating. "Once you know the key, you can apply it to the cipher and read the hidden message. Maybe '3' is the key to a quick cipher Kairoth came up with. He expected Ember would take special notice of the number three because it is incorrect, as he well knew. So, what is the simplest cipher he could have used? I think a substitution cipher."

The gnome fell silent. Hennet flushed with mild jealousy—he was the one who liked puzzles, yet Nebin was apparently well versed in such things. Hennett had never heard of a substitution cipher.

Growing more excited as he was drawn into the puzzle's challenge, Nebin continued, "A popular cipher uses only the first letter of each sentence to spell out a secret message. But every gnome child knows that one. Perhaps the message is secretly spelled out using every third letter of each sentence? Hmm . . ." He quickly ran his finger along the text and read, "She . . . emmso . . . lie . . . ŏsi."

"Gibberish," said Brek Gorunn, and Hennet had to agree.

"Wait, maybe it is the third letter from the end of each sentence!" The gnome began reading backward, but quickly came up with the same sort of nonsense.

Brek Gorunn shook his head. Nebin's face fell. They all stood glumly looking at the letter.

Hennet cleared his throat and offered, "Does the number three have any meaning if you apply it somehow to the doodles?"

He still felt the random letters were important, but this whole business of ciphers was new to him.

Nebin ran his fingers along the smudged letters. He said, "The letters are 'phhwphlqwkhwhpsoh.' If it is a substitution cipher, it could be that each letter here is actually three letters farther along in the alphabet of the language used for the coded message. I would assume that's the same language used in the rest of the letter."

The gnome hunched over the table, grabbed an inked quill from those he was using earlier, and muttered under his breath as he wrote on the back of the letter.

"Right, that would give us 'skkzskot znkzksvrk.'" The gnome scratched his beard. "Still nothing."

Ember broke in, "Try it the other direction." She leaned forward, eager to see the gnome's handiwork.

Nebin paused, then slowly wrote, one letter at a time, "mee tme int het emp le."

Hennet drew in his breath quickly. Despite his feeling about the doodles, he was surprised when he was vindicated. There was a secret message!

Nebin said, "Hennet, we should have listened to you right off.

It says, 'Meet me in the temple.' Kairoth didn't want anyone to read this but you, Ember!"

Ember clapped Hennet and the gnome on the back and said, "I have been traveling with masters of secrets all this time. How did you know?"

Hennet shrugged and smiled.

Nebin absorbed the praise and responded, "As I said, gnomes like ciphers. We learn them as games in our childhood. Now you know our secret. Well, actually, only gnome children would use ciphers as simple as this, but humans have to start somewhere."

The gnome laughed and twirled his inked quill.

"Kairoth can only mean the temple he talked about in the main message," said Ember.

"Then let us prepare to venture below the city," declared Brek Gorunn, ever practical.

"When Baron Dammeral founded New Koratia four hundred years ago, I wonder if he knew about the ancient city that once stood here?" wondered Nebin.

Hennet, Ember, Brek Gorunn, and Nebin trudged through a sewer tunnel. They had prepared and rested for most of the previous night, then started before dawn. Even though Hennet and Nebin had a free day before the first round of the Duel Arcane, Ember wondered if the two shouldn't be practicing their magic. She felt guilty for asking them along. She suspected that Hennet had something of a crush on her, and she hoped she wasn't trading on that affection. On the other hand, Ember presumed that Nebin tagged along on the jaunt into the sewers because of his relentless overconfidence.

"What ancient city, Nebin?" asked Ember.

The wizard enjoyed showing off his knowledge and she didn't mind indulging him.

"The city of New Koratia was established when the original city of Koratia burned in The Conflagration of Tael." The ruins of

Old Koratia still sat, fifteen miles to the south, where the River Delnir emptied into the Southern Sea. "Actually, even back then the ancient city was a ruin, its name lost," continued Nebin, a pedantic edge creeping into his voice. "It was only discovered because of a few surface collapses when Dammeral began building, revealing an old tunnel system. Dammeral thought the tunnels would provide a perfect foundation for a 'modern' sewer."

Ember remembered hearing something like that when she'd earlier lived in New Koratia. She also knew that the tunnels were rumored to be part of an ancient temple complex dedicated to an infernal god. The monk decided to keep that tidbit to herself if the gnome didn't already know it. Nebin had proved a bit flighty, and she didn't want to cultivate his fear. Anyway, she didn't think they had much to worry about. Overall, the tunnels made good sewer conduits.

The stench was palpable. Nebin was most affected by the odor. He claimed it was because, being the shortest, his head was closest to the liquid that swirled down the center of the brick tunnel. Soon enough, however, they left the sewers and their stink behind, as they entered the older, pre-Koratian tunnels. Brek Gorunn carried a lantern, though he carried it only out of courtesy—as a dwarf, he could find his way in the dark without aid from artificial light.

Ember provided directions, drawing on the memories of her previous trek. The tunnel turned a few times then sloped downward. At times they felt cooler air on their faces, issuing from dark, side passages. Though they saw many branching corridors—some with stairs, some narrow, and others broad—Ember kept to the passage originally selected, which continued to lead steadily but gradually down.

The corridor finally emptied into a broad hall. Besides the passage they arrived on, two other tunnels departed the hall.

Directly opposite them was a high, wide arch scribed with many runes. Heavy stone doors, likewise scribbled with signs—or perhaps graffiti—barred passage, but one of the doors was slightly ajar.

"This is the place Kairoth and I found during our expedition," said Ember. She was relieved to have found it so easily. "We translated the runes on the arch and door as best we could. They speak of reverence for the unseen, sacrifice, and power. We dubbed it a temple, though I suppose it could be something else. We never got past the doors."

"They're open now," observed Brek Gorunn. "Where is Kairoth? Perhaps he got tired of waiting."

The dwarf moved forward to examine the stonework of the arch, nodding in appreciation.

Where was he, indeed? Ember wondered.

She didn't let her uncertainty color her features or voice when she said, "Perhaps he only checks this place periodically. He may have left a message."

She began searching the floor of the hall near the arch. Nebin and Hennet joined her. The light of the lantern held by the dwarf cast their shadows long across the floor of the chamber and up into the narrow tunnels.

"Here," said Hennet. Ember saw that the sorcerer squatted near one corner. "A ring of stones. Looks like a fire ring, and used recently."

Hennet reached into the pit and disturbed a layer of ash.

Ember and Brek Gorunn joined the sorcerer. The dwarf pointed.

"See the scratches here, as if something was dragged? Dragged through this archway, unless I miss my mark. Whoever camped here either decided to go exploring, or something inside the 'temple' came out and got him."

"Him . . ." mused Ember, her heart beating faster. "You think it was Kairoth?"

"Who else?" said Brek. "Based on his message, he should be here. Here, we find signs of a camp and an ambush."

Ember couldn't find fault with the dwarf's logic.

She nodded and said, "Then, through the arch we go. Be wary."

Ember strolled over to the arch, but the sight of one of the runes on the door distracted her. It strongly resembled the strange symbol she'd seen on Elder Vobod's ring—a circle with many arrows pointing inward. She hoped it was merely coincidence. She could do nothing about it except push on.

Ember worked her fingers into the crack between the cold, wet door and frame and pulled. She had to place her foot against the wall and strain before being rewarded with the sounds of creaking hinges and stone grating against stone, but at last the portal moved and swung wide.

She looked to her companions and asked, "Everyone ready?"

Hennet unslung his crossbow. He cranked back the mechanism and loaded it with a bolt.

"I thought you preferred magic?" she asked him.

"In a tight spot, I prefer options."

Ember laughed, hoping to break the tension that had descended at the sight of the chamber beyond the portal.

Brek's lantern revealed that, unlike the crude stonework of the tunnels they stood in, the newly revealed chamber was tiled in a greenish-brown stone. A pile of ash, broken bones, stony debris, and unidentifiable filth lay heaped in the room's center. The smell of rot, as of food too long in the sun, made Ember's nose wrinkle. A single passage led farther into the complex. Nothing moved, save dust particles in the beam of light.

"Hold back a moment, let me go first," said Ember.

The rest of the group didn't argue. She knew she had a knack for taking charge, but after all, they were there because of her. She walked slowly forward, looking around as she went, moving toward the ash heap. She didn't like its shape, but something glinted on top.

Ember was about halfway between the arch and the heap when the tile below her gave way. One side of the tile flipped down as if on a hinge. She dropped down into the pit without a sound and was gone.

"Ember!" yelled Hennet, sprinting into the room.

He wasn't the only one yelling or entering the room. Two figures issued from the shadowed hallway opposite the ash heap, shuffling and shambling forward. Hennet stopped short of the pit Ember had fallen into, his eyes wide, and his hands clenched in determination. The mere sight of the creatures threatened to send him spiraling into mind-numbing despair, but he fought it back.

The creatures were withered and desiccated, their features hidden beneath centuries-old funerary wrappings. They moved with a steady gait, heading toward the edge of the pit Ember had fallen into. A pungent order wafted forward, like that of a spice cabinet left too long without cleaning.

Hennet spared a glance at his companions. True to form, the gnome looked terrified beyond any capacity for casting spells. Brek appeared less affected, but still taken aback.

The dwarf whispered, "Mummified corpses! 'Ware their touch; it's deadly."

Hennet nodded. He stowed his crossbow and prepared to cast a spell. He hoped that, as a cleric, Brek had power over unlife like other priests he'd known.

Brek Gorunn took a step forward, held forth his hammer, and bellowed, "Moradin commands that you give way, unholy creatures! Turn your faces and be destroyed!"

His hammer blazed with golden light and one of the two advancing mummies faltered, croaked out a terrible whine, and turned back toward the way it had come. The other shook off Brek's holy command and continued forward, reaching the edge of the pit.

Not so fast, thought Hennet.

He summoned a duo of enchanted force missiles from his outstretched hand, which slammed into the creature like hurled daggers. It absorbed the magical attack with barely a shudder, despite two bloodless holes smoking in its torso. It kept advancing.

Desperate, Hennet yelled, "Your wand! Nebin, your wand!"

Hennet silently cursed as the gnome remained frozen in fear. Not so Brek, who rushed forward swinging his warhammer. But he moved too slowly for Hennet's taste. The animate corpse was leaning forward and straining with one arm to reach down into the pit. Hennet released another twin barrage of magical energy; the thing shuddered again, but still remained on its feet.

"Damn you, Nebin!" yelled the human sorcerer, "wake up and use your wand!"

The gnome groaned and grasped the slender wooden wand at his belt with shaking hands. Its touch seemed to lend Nebin confidence. He whipped out the wand and aimed its tip at the mummified corpse.

"Back to dust with you!" Nebin shrilled, and released a cascade of rainbow light fully onto the stooping creature.

The color drained away, leaving the creature unfazed. It groped around below the lip of the pit, chuffing in anticipation.

Nebin groaned, "Mindless husk!" and dropped his wand to the floor.

The mummy straightened, hauling Ember out of the pit. It held her firmly around the neck with one arm. The monk struggled and kicked, but she was already hurt from her fall. Long-dead tendons tensed as the creature squeezed, and Ember's struggles weakened. What blows and kicks she landed had little effect on the creature. Hennet realized it was going to squeeze the life from her before their eyes!

The dwarf charged around the edge of the pit and accelerated toward the thing. The mummy looked up just in time to take Brek's hammer full in the face. The creature was already shot through with smoking holes from Hennet's magical assault. It uttered a dusty sigh then collapsed, inert. Its hold on Ember relaxed; the monk dropped back into the pit.

Hennet was right behind the dwarf, but he arrived too late to grab the flailing monk before she fell for the second time. He rushed up to the edge of the pit, his heart in his mouth.

"Thank Pelor," muttered Hennet when he saw her hanging on the lip of the pit, struggling to hold on but still breathing.

"Lend me a hand, will you?" she said in a husky voice.

Minutes later, refreshed by the cleric's healing spells, including a ward against disease, Ember returned to the ash heap and plucked the shining thing from its top.

"This is Kairoth's ring. The inscription reads 'Enabled Hand.' He was in this chamber!" she proclaimed. "We must press on."

"I was hoping we'd retreat," worried Nebin.

Hennet laughed and said, "A mighty arcane warrior you are, Nebin! Let the undead tremble at your approach."

Nebin looked miffed. He said, looking at Ember, "I'm only suggesting possibilities. Of course I want to continue!"

"Thanks," said Ember. "Now let's find Kairoth, or those who stole him away. I must be sure of his fate."

Her comrades all nodded. Time to press on.

Ember and the dwarf moved up to the mouth of the passage from which the mummies had emerged. Brek's lantern revealed the same greenish-brown stone tiling the passage. Carved niches broke the plane of both walls lining the corridor. Some contained urns, others were empty.

Ember motioned everyone forward, whispering, "Don't touch the urns. Best not to disturb the dead."

She moved forward cautiously, her companions padding along behind as silently as they could. She gave each niche with an urn a wide berth. A breath of colder air tugged her hair.

A whisper behind her said, "Dim your lantern. I see light." It was Nebin.

Brek obliged the gnome. In the utter darkness of the passage, Ember saw a greenish glow ahead. The illumination trickled from around a bend in the corridor. The colder air brought with it the sound of a low, guttural chanting, barely discernable.

Ember immediately moved forward, resolute. After a few seconds of hesitation, she heard the others follow her. She was relieved—she had half expected at least the gnome to bolt, and the others to try to argue her back.

When she reached the bend, Ember peered around. The corridor opened into a domed room, from which many exits led into darkness. A head-sized ball of green fire hung high in the air at the center of the dome, glaring with emerald light. Below the ghoul-glow, a figure half bound in funerary wrappings lay draped across a chipped stone altar. A hideous, animate, mummified corpse stood next to the altar chanting in a harsh, breathless, uncouth voice, and jerking its arms around as if casting a spell. The chanting mummy wore an elaborate headdress and clutched a blood-stained scythe in one hand.

Ember recognized a mortal threat when she saw one. Without giving herself a second to consider running, she rushed the mummified chanter. It was a simple decision—she recognized the figure on the altar as her old mentor, Kairoth. She leaped onto the altar, readying a lethal kick.

The chanting cut off as if severed by a knife. The scythe came around, whistling in a vicious arc. Faster than Ember could respond, her armored forearm rose, deflecting the lethal blow. The motion surprised even her. Then she realized—Loku's Bracer had awakened and revealed its magical legacy. The mummy would have disemboweled her as she leaped onto the altar without the bracers' aid. She mouthed silent thanks to Loku, wherever his spirit resided.

With her height advantage atop the altar, Ember struck with *shi kune*, the "stunning fist," executing it perfectly. The mummy's head rocked back, then snapped forward instantly, unfazed. Apparently the walking dead were not easily stunned, Ember scolded herself.

Hearing the beat of many footfalls, she glanced back and saw the others finally rushing to her aid with Brek Gorunn in the lead. The dwarf, his legs pumping, ran around the left side of the altar, brandishing his hammer.

Ember punched and chopped at the creature's head, trying to dislodge the grinning rictus from its mummified torso. The dead creature stepped back from Ember's flashing fists, moving beyond her reach from atop the altar. It pointed a single finger at the approaching dwarf and coughed forth a stream of acid syllables. An ominous ray erupted from its wrapped finger, striking the dwarf in the chest. Brek exhaled as if punched in the stomach, then groaned. The dwarf sank to his knees, as if suddenly too weak to support his own weight.

The mummified chanter had Ember's full attention. She heard Hennet and Nebin incanting spells behind her. Nebin's voice finished first—his spell called forth a brilliant reddish orb that thundered into the mummy. It grunted, but did not fall.

Ember got the attention of the creature with a solid kick to its head. It rocked back, more by the force of the blow than from pain, which Ember doubted it could even feel.

Hennet's voice finally ceased with an exultant lilt. Ember looked back again to see what the sorcerer had wrought. A deadly certainty seemed to infuse him. He brought his crossbow to his shoulder in a liquid moment and fired. Magic guided his hands, and the bolt sped true, burying itself deeply into the chest of the mummy. The creature, which had begun mouthing a new, foul incantation, screeched and stepped back another pace. Its spell fizzled and was wasted.

Ember saw her chance to end the conflict. She jumped into the air, spinning with deadly force. Her right foot kicked out and connected. The force of her jump, spin, and kick slammed instantly into the mummy, and snapped its brittle body in half. The torso, ripped open at the waist, tumbled to the floor. It was followed moments later by the collapsing legs. Small trinkets and other oddments scattered, apparently shaken loose from the creature's wrappings. It lay in a heap, unmoving save for a puff of grave dust that rose from its hollow interior.

Ember remained wary, ready in case other threats should materialize. Hennet reslung his light crossbow and rushed over to Brek. The dwarf put his back to the altar. He was breathing shallowly.

"What did he hex you with?" asked Hennet.

"I'm not certain. I'm as weak as a newborn. Not something a dwarf likes to admit."

Ember turned to the half-wrapped man on the altar, feeling for a pulse, and found it. There was no mistake, it was Kairoth, and he still lived. Heartened, she gently shook him. His eyelids fluttered, then closed again. He whispered a few words before lapsing back into unconsciousness.

Ember turned to the others and said, "The elder requires tending. He is sorely wounded." She shot an inquisitive look at the dwarf, but Brek shook his head, to say Brek Gorunn needed tending, too. "Very well, we have what we came for. It's time to go. Moradin willing, Brek Gorunn will shake off the curse by the morrow."

She lifted her old mentor as if he weighed no more than a child.

Ember called to Nebin, who remained standing near the entrance, "When I finished off the mummy, I shook lose a few rings and scrolls. You may want to take a look."

The gnome's expression turned from diffidence to eager anticipation as he rushed forward.

She turned to Hennet and said, "Watch for more creatures as we retreat. At least one more lurks nearby, the one Brek Gorunn chased away."

Hennet nodded, but continued to look at Kairoth, draped in Ember's arms.

"What did he say, when you woke him?" the sorcerer asked.

"I'm not sure," responded Ember. "Something about 'the Oath'."

The Duel Arcane was the biggest event in New Koratia. Held every three years, it afforded the city a wonderful influx of business as wizards, sorcerers, hedge wizards, shamans, and not a few charlatans and fakirs descended on the city. Inns were full, and business in the bazaar was brisk. Outfitters of all types expected booming sales. The city welcomed the wizards with open arms (especially particularly famous, and rich, mages). Many shops and temporary carts greatly expanded their magical inventory of reagents, arcane focuses, ingredients, and spell components while the duel ran. Inflated prices for especially rare components was a form of profiteering expected by every attending mage.

Hennet and Nebin approached the coliseum beneath the Floating Crystal, which hovered like a solid cloud. This time, the press of people on the streets was almost impassable. Everyone with an interest in the duel moved toward the half-bowl seating, and that seemed to include most of the city. In fact, a holiday atmosphere was evident. Sweetmeat vendors with tiny carts were everywhere hawking delicious snacks. Children rode on their parents' shoulders as they moved toward the coliseum while apprentice mages not much older, apparently from the college itself, passed out minor charms and firecrackers. The crowd was primed and excited to see the magical contest.

With the help of green-robed duel officials—wizards from the sponsoring College of Wizardry—Hennet and Nebin made it through the press to the edge of the field where dozens of other competitor mages waited. The stands were full. Thousands of people yelled, cheered, talked, and screamed. The crowd came to see magic, and they would not be disappointed.

Over thirty "casting circles" were marked out on the field, denoted by colored stones. Nebin guessed that each circular area was twenty feet across. Most of the casting circles already contained dueling mages. Each duel was attended by a judge in green robes. Clerics of Pelor, a beneficent deity, stood along the sidelines, ready to grant the grace of healing to those who lost a bout particularly badly. Flashes, explosions, strange smells, phantoms, and summoned beasts ran riot in and around the field.

Nebin was so excited that it felt as if his hair was standing on end—perhaps because of all the magic in the air, he thought. He raised his arms, trying to feel the magical flux. A blast of energy nearby hurled a man in a camel-brown suit from a ring. He'd lost his match to a woman in silvery clothing, but Nebin missed the spell she'd used to send her opponent sprawling. A duel was over when one contestant was magically forced out of his circle, either directly or indirectly, or if a judge called the bout one way or the other after a preset amount of time. If even part of the competitor's body left the circle, the bout was over. Losers did not advance in the competition. Nebin mentally promised himself, for the hundredth time, that he would not be a loser.

The gnome felt a tap on his own shoulder.

"Nebin Raulnor?" a judge said. "You're up. Come with me."

Hennet gave him the thumbs up sign for good luck. The gnome gulped.

Nebin followed the judge, who wore the symbol of the Floating Crystal, out to a casting circle near the center of the field. Already a diaphanously robed human woman stood in the circle, her eyes closed and hands clasped. Close up, the gnome could see that the circles were already scored and discolored from earlier spells. The judge ushered him into the circle. Sand and gravel crunched beneath his feet as he walked to his position.

Nebin greeted his opponent with a pleasant, "Hello!"

She narrowed her eyes.

So that's how she wants to play it, he thought.

"Nebin Raulnor," called out the judge in a remarkably loud voice, "wizard, novice, faces off against Filiseethra, wizard, novice. You have three minutes to duel, and they begin . . . *now!*"

Wh-what, now? mentally stuttered the gnome.

He tried to ignore the increasingly boisterous crowd, which was easier than ignoring the magical flashes and booms of other matches.

Like a striking snake, his opponent Filiseethra grabbed a wand from her belt and pointed it toward him. He cursed himself, just then remembering that wands and lesser magical items were allowed! Her wand crackled, and a cold wind surged against him. Outside the casting circle it was little more than a breeze, but against Nebin, it was a gale. The wind pushed him back toward the circle's edge. He leaned into it, trying to brace his feet against the rough ground, but he continued sliding. His goggles protected his eyes from the blowing sand, and he was thankful he'd remembered to pull them down. The woman, her wand outthrust, slowly advanced.

Nebin carefully felt for his own wand. With the wind interfering, he doubted he could cast a spell, but not so the wand's power. The woman's eyes widened as he brought it up and pointed it at her.

Not so tricksy, now, eh? thought the gnome, as a stream of flashing, multicolored light flashed from the wand and into Filiseethra's face.

She gasped, throwing one forearm across her eyes.

The wind abated instantly, and Nebin stumbled forward. His competitor groaned, then fell face forward into the sand.

"The bout goes to Nebin Raulnor!" exclaimed the judge.

The woman, unable to see anything but swirling colors, was pulled from the circle by a Peloran cleric. Nebin strutted to his next match.

Hennet's first competitor was a salt-bearded fellow called Harper. Harper stood in the circle across from Hennet, darting glances to and fro. Sweat beaded on his brow, and he rubbed his hands incessantly. Hennet's own nervousness faded somewhat on seeing his competitor so shaken. He restrained himself from offering the man encouragement. This was a competition, after all.

". . . begin *now!*" bawled out the judge.

Hennet was ready. A puff of sulfurous smoke from a nearby magical duel half-occluded Harper, who actually mewled in terror.

What's up with this guy? wondered Hennet.

Rather than attacking his already intimidated opponent all-out, he decided to gamble on conserving power for a later match. Hennet opened his mouth and crooned a whispery sound. Infused by magic from his waving fingertips, the sound was transformed. A low growl, as of a lion catching scent of its prey, issued from the center of the hazy circle. When Hennet heard the man take in a deep breath, he knew he'd won already. As his hands moved farther apart, the low growl increased in volume, quickly becoming the ear-shattering roar of a charging lion!

The judge stepped back, nearby competitors stumbled in the midst of their spells, and Harper wet himself as he fell out of the circle. The round was Hennett's. Even better, he'd won with the first spell that he ever mastered, one that stole into his mind on the eve of his thirteenth birthday. He'd used it often since then, but never before with such perfection. It was going to be a good day.

Walking to his second match, Nebin realized something important. In order to win the last matches of the day, he'd need to conserve spells and tricks. The more spells and wand energy he used early, the less he would have available for the final match. And, logically, each new opponent would be more challenging than the ones who came before, as the weakest were weeded out first. Nebin glanced around, looking for Hennet. He wanted to share his revelation, but the constant flash and dazzle of spells restricted his view to only the closest duels.

His next opponent was a diminutive elf, nearly as short as Nebin. The elf wore a simple tunic the color of rose petals. Nebin pegged him as an apprentice who'd recently learned his first real spell, and gave a smug smile calculated to infuriate. Then the duel commenced.

Ready this time, Nebin whipped out his wand and fired off two blasts of rioting color before the elf could do more than blink.

When the color faded, the elf blinked a second time and said quietly, "I'm immune to that enchantment. Are you?"

The elf raised one hand as if cupping something and lobbed it underhand at the gnome. Halfway between the elf and Nebin, the unseen something ignited with a violet *whumpf!* A sphere of burning purple the size of his head slammed into Nebin. Pain flared through him, unexpected and unbearable. He was certain that his body would be gushing blood from a thousand wounds but for the cauterizing effect of the fiery sphere that was consuming his flesh. Nebin scrambled back, and the sphere fell and bounced away. Gasping for breath, Nebin saw that the elf held one hand forward, gently waving his fingertips. The gnome's breath came even quicker when he saw the sphere respond to the elf's gestures and roll back toward him.

At that moment, Nebin believed with all his might that anything, death included, would be better than being touched by that sphere again. He was so desperate to avoid it that the simplest solution, stepping out of the circle, never occurred to him. Instead, he began breathlessly reciting a long string of harsh syllables. The burning sphere rolled around the periphery of the circle toward him, and Nebin lurched frantically away, trying to stay ahead of it. Walking and casting spells simultaneously was difficult even for arch wizards, let alone someone who hovered just beyond death's grasp. The gnome moved and incanted, chanted and dodged, laboring through magical verses that were far too complex for such a competition. All the while, the sphere narrowed the gap. He could feel the heat groping toward him. Nebin, the sphere, and the elf all moved around the inside of the circle as if pantomiming the face of a sundial.

Nebin smiled as he gasped out the final syllables of his spell. The elf looked confused for a moment when nothing happened, then a shadow swept across his face. He looked up just in time to meet the talons of a stooping hawk with hell-bright eyes. As the hawk raked bloody tracks across the elf's face, its scream was matched by the elf's.

"Not my face!" he shrieked, throwing his hands across his eyes.

Nebin leaped into the air when he saw the flaming sphere dissipate. The hawk that he had summoned from an otherworldly place to do his bidding flapped, screeched, and tore at the elf's arms and head.

Nebin laughed, screaming, "Who's immune now, elf?"

The elf turned and ran, the hawk bedeviling him as he scurried across the floor of the coliseum. Nebin stepped into an impromptu jig but the burning pain in his side stopped him cold.

He called, "Healing!" and a priest moved forward, the sunburst of Pelor on his mantle.

He ran his hands over Nebin's sides. Where he touched, the blackened flesh turned supple and brown.

Then the priest gave Nebin a chiding look as he walked away, saying, "Be not too swift to call dark agents to your side, lest you become addicted to their hate. Seek instead for allies in the celestial sphere."

Nebin ducked his head guiltily. True, the hawk had the taint of the Lower Planes on it, but his choices were limited. He did what he needed to win the match and refused to believe that was wrong. It was only a game, after all. But despite his rationalizations, Nebin also knew the priest's words were true. He promised himself he'd remember the warning.

He turned to the standings, which flashed on a large, blank wall in magical glyphs. In the Novice Competition, two rounds remained for those who advanced. Nebin knew that after that, there would be a few days before the finals. The novices competing for the Golden Wand had to wait for the intermediate and grandmaster competitions. But the boards revealed wonderful news: He was getting a bye into the last round! The gnome wondered what he had done that fate was so kind to him. He took the ten minutes at his disposal to wander the field, looking for Hennet. Had the sorcerer already lost? He couldn't find his friend, but did find Aganon, the spellcaster they'd met during the preliminaries.

Nebin called, "Aganon! How fares the day?"

Aganon looked up, saw the gnome, and bragged, "I am at the top of my magic. Stay, and learn a thing or two."

Aganon certainly is sure of himself. Sort of like me, realized the gnome.

Aganon faced off against a dwarf with snow-white braids in his beard and a short, stout staff inset with a crystal. The dwarf aimed a narrow fan of fire at Aganon, who ducked most of it, but not all. Nebin saw a Peloran cleric move closer, monitoring Aganon's fight, along with another match in the next ring where ice bolts were haphazardly flung. Aganon palmed a vial and gulped it down. Suddenly, he burst into frenzied motion, vibrating with quickness. He moved so fast that his movements blurred. The dwarf's eyes narrowed with understanding, and he fumbled for something at his belt. Aganon's form began running around the periphery of the ring, completing a circuit in less than a second. With each circuit, he tightened his course, coming ever closer to the worried dwarf.

The dwarf pulled out a scroll, reading aloud the inscribed runes. A yellow ray flashed away from one of the dwarf's gesturing hands, striking the blurred figure of Aganon. Aganon stumbled. He flailed, cried out, and ran straight into the dwarf. The force of the impact knocked the dwarf completely out of the ring onto his back. Aganon was down, too. Even sprawled out as he was, Nebin saw that Aganon remained completely inside the circle. He struggled back to his feet, gradually blurring back to normal speed.

Aganon turned his head toward Nebin and gave the gnome a secret wink, whispering, "All's fair in the duel, eh Nebin?"

"Foul!" cried the dwarf. "He pushed me out! Disqualify him. That wasn't magic."

Aganon looked indignant, saying, "My worthy competitor jokes! I fell, as all could see. It was his ray that caused me to stumble, and he knows it. Besides, I was moving under the influence of an enchantment of acceleration. If striking the dwarf forced him from the circle, it was because the force was magically multiplied."

The judge conferred with another, and after a few seconds, one called, "The bout goes to Aganon!"

The dwarf mage scowled, rattled off a few choice Dwarvish words, and stalked away. Aganon glanced at Nebin again, giving the gnome a satisfied smirk. Several people in the crowd gave a cheer, chanting, "Aganon! Aganon!"

Nebin didn't know how to react. He felt a little strange at witnessing the trick the man had played, if it was a trick. Maybe it was a reasonable, if sneaky, tactic? Before he could make any comment to Aganon, a duel official from across the field called Nebin's name. It was the last round of the day.

Aganon called to him as he moved off, "I will see you, Nebin!"

Feeling vaguely unsettled, the gnome nodded, moving toward his final round.

He thought his final opponent of the day might be a human woman, though her skin had a faint, reddish color. Not that he could see much of it; she was completely wrapped in a shawl of white. She held a slender staff inlaid with runes of glowing pearl. Magical rings clinked on her fingers, and at her belt were girt three wands. Nebin had a sinking sensation. He pulled his goggles down over his eyes.

The judge called, ""Nebin Raulnor, wizard, novice, faces off against the White Enchantress, novice. You have three minutes to duel, and they begin . . . *now!*"

Nebin fumbled for his wand.

For her part, the White Enchantress beamed a glorious smile at Nebin, and said, "Wouldn't you like to be my very best friend?"

Her eyes sparked with beguilement. And Nebin realized, that yes, indeed, he would like that, very much. He would do much to please this woman, if only she would tell him her desire. He pushed his wand firmly back into place on his belt. The woman smiled more broadly, if possible.

"You're a wonderful little man, aren't you? I can tell we are going to be the best of friends. I have only a small request, between friends. I am so parched! Please, be a dear and fetch me a dipper of water from over there, would you?"

Well, of course he would go get his friend a dipper of water! She was his very best friend, wasn't she? He laughed, pleased by the absurdity of her request. As if he would refuse her. He began walking to the edge of the casting circle.

"Nebin! Wake up! What are you doing?"

Nebin stopped, looking for who spoke. It was Hennet. The gnome was delighted. He would introduce his old friend Hennet to his newest friend, the White Enchantress. A pretty name, that.

Nebin called to Hennet, "I was looking for you earlier. How'd you do? Oh never mind, that can wait; I want to introduce you to the White Enchantress. Isn't she extraordinary?" Nebin finished with a sappy grin.

The judge watched the discussion with an incredulous look on his face. Nebin wondered why.

Hennet shook his head. "Think about what you just said; she's an enchantress! You're in the middle of a match, right now! If you fetch her a dipper of water, you leave the circle, and she wins.

What kind of friend would ask you to do that? She's enchanted you, and you'd better shake it off, or you're done."

Nebin pushed his goggles up onto his forehead. Hennet had a point.

He turned back to the Enchantress and asked, "Can I get you that dipper after we're done here?"

Her smile turned to a frown, and she growled, "You're useless! Why would I ever be your friend? Never speak to me again."

The effect of her words on the gnome was immediate. He wilted, hanging his head. Tears of shame welled in his eyes. He had forgotten what it felt like to be rejected. No, he hadn't forgotten, it just had never felt this bad before. Maybe if he explained . . . He looked up and saw that the White Enchantress held one her wands.

She aimed it and said, "Maybe this will make you feel better, poor guy."

A stupid grin stretched Nebin's lips as a spray of color showered from her wand, washing over him in a buzz of conflicting urges. How could she use his favorite spell against him? What kind of friend would do that? Realization hit him as he tried shaking off the flashing colors. Hennet called it right; she'd enchanted him. But the charm was broken.

A rush of words tumbled from his mouth, long and loud. The spell was lengthy but had worked to great effect earlier. He had a moment of doubt, remembering the priest's words. Should he avoid that spell, try something else? No, time was running out and he needed a powerful distraction. The White Enchantress tried to ensorcel him once more, but he shut his ears to her entreaties. She wouldn't humiliate him twice in a row.

He chanted the last syllable. A roll of noise, like thunder, heralded the appearance of a red-feathered bird of prey. It materialized right next to the White Enchantress. Its beak was stained with blood, and its eyes shone with the fury of Hell. Then it was on her.

The White Enchantress gave ground, crying aloud. The fiendish hawk went for her eyes, beak pecking and talons scratching.

"Forfeit! I forfeit! Get it away," she yelled.

Nebin had hoped only to confuse her with the summoned creature so he could force her out of the ring in some other fashion, but this was even better. With a snap, he dismissed the spell; the cruel raptor faded away, leaving only a wisp of smoke.

The White Enchantress, with the creature gone, regained her composure, though her face remained flushed.

She said to Nebin, "You are a worthy competitor. Good luck to you."

Then she walked away, still the image of poise. Despite himself, Nebin felt a small echo of friendliness toward her. She possessed potent magic, and he hoped he would see her again.

Hennet clapped the gnome on the shoulders and said, "That's it, we're both in. I had a bye this last round; my first three rounds were laughable. I faced one mage named Harper who didn't even manage to cast a spell. I wish you had seen him quaking in fear. Well, it's done. We're both in the finals!"

The judge called out Nebin's win. Hennet and Nebin cheered, as did a contingent in the crowd. Apparently, one or both of them had picked up a small following. It was a good day for dueling.

The mages returned to the Cuttlestone Inn, triumphant. After a drink in the common room, they repaired to their quarters. Hennet felt a flush of guilt when he recalled the predicament of Ember, Brek, and the injured elder. They remained behind in the mages' room while Hennet and Nebin competed in the Duel Arcane.

Hennet knocked, then pushed open the door to their room. "What news?" he called.

Kairoth lay on a cot near the window, propped up with pillows. Ember sat on a stool next to him. The two were in the midst of speaking, but Ember looked up and smiled at Hennet. He realized the smile was the first of real sincerity he had seen from the monk. It's warmth sent a shiver of excitement thrilling through him.

Yes, I have it bad, he cajoled himself.

Brek Gorunn sat at the small table that was now piled with scrolls, a ring, and other oddments they had taken from the mummified creature below the city.

He said, "We're better, thanks to Moradin's grace. How fared your duel?"

Nebin pushed past the sorcerer and said, "Could you expect any less than total victory? Hennet's foes were slipshod; their magic was weak. He could have called light and won his duels. In fact, I think that's exactly what he did at least once. But me! I faced such challenges! Why, one evil shrew took direct control of my mind. If not for a supreme effort of will—something I've practiced—I'd still be in her power. I'm surprised they let someone so awesome compete at our level."

"A supreme effort of will and my help, you mean," interjected Hennet.

"Right, I was coming to that."

"In any case," continued Hennet, "we're both slated for the finals in two days. But, what about you?" He fixed the man on the cot with his direct gaze, saying, "It's a pleasure to make your acquaintance Elder Kairoth. Ember speaks well of you."

Kairoth's hair was shaved, his features chiseled as if from granite, and he had a wiry build. He wore a ring on one hand, the same ring Ember retrieved from the pile of ashes in the temple.

Ember said, "Elder Kairoth, please tell them what you've told us. These are the two who helped us find and retrieve you from below the city."

The man weighed Hennet, then Nebin, with a look. Apparently, they passed.

The man said, "It is good to make your acquaintance, young friends. You have my deepest gratitude. You have allowed one last chance for redemption for the Enabled Hand."

Kairoth sat up straighter and took a drink from a small cup.

"Brek Gorunn has healed me of my physical hurts," he continued, "but I remain spiritually weakened, for now. My life energy was nearly snuffed out. Others were not saved as I was.

The Order was betrayed."

"Betrayed?" asked the gnome.

"I will start at the beginning. Five weeks ago, a student of mine, Adeva Silverhair, disappeared. At first it seemed nothing, but when a search of her quarters revealed the possibility of foul play, I became concerned. It seemed as if there had been a struggle, and I found blood. I was especially distraught because I scolded Adeva for her impudence earlier that day. Perhaps my harsh words left her open to poor choices. I do not know.

"Regardless, when I went to Elder Vobod and told him of Adeva's disappearance, he laughed. He said Adeva had merely gone away on a trip. Then he gave me a terrible look, and told me that if I didn't want to see where she'd gone, I'd better forget about it. Can you imagine, an elder threatening another? That was when I penned my message to Ember. I hid a secret message in the letter, in case the courier was intercepted."

Ember shook her head. "And I completely missed it. I took the message at face value."

Kairoth touched her shoulder. "You deciphered the message when you needed to."

The elder continued his story. "That night, there was an attack. Fully ten of the fifteen instructors and three of the quorum of five elders turned on the rest. Vobod led them, though he referred to some mysterious, greater power. I escaped because I was already on my guard from Vobod's earlier theatrics. The attacks were constrained to the instructors' wing—no students or novices were involved. They may not know that the order is now in the hands of a malevolent force."

"How can they not know?" asked Hennet.

"Because the students, while they might be curious about the terrible ruckus in the night, would never dishonor an instructor with questions about things that were not their business."

"Who were the elders you spoke with, Ember?" asked Hennet. He worried to think of her having set foot in the place, if what Kairoth said was true.

Ember shuddered. "Vobod himself. You see, I knew he had lied to me."

Brek said, "Could Vobod's uprising have anything to do with what happened in Ember's chapter? There, it was red-masked cultists who serve Nerull."

"Yes, red-masked cultists who seemed strangely proficient in martial crafts," mused Ember.

"Unsettling. Why is the Order of the Enabled Hand consuming itself from the inside?" questioned Kairoth.

"I'll help you find out," promised Ember.

Brek nodded his aid.

"Kairoth, how did you end up below the city?" asked Nebin.

"Ember and I discovered those doors years ago. The designs I remembered on the entrance to the temple matched the symbols carried by Vobod on his ring. I thought it would be profitable to examine them more closely. I didn't expect to be attacked down there. Had I known that evil was awake in that old sanctuary of death, I would have chosen a safer place for Ember and I to rendezvous."

Ember sighed. "What can we do now?"

"Because Vobod is a respected elder, he can deny any claim we make concerning his illegitimacy," said Kairoth. "It will be our word against his."

Hennet steeled himself and said, "Then we must find out the truth. It is up to us to see justice done."

"Us?" asked Ember. "This is not your fight; you have your duel. You've already aided us more than is right. I feel bad enough for that, though without your help Kairoth could well be dead."

Hennet shook his head. "I'd like to think that we have all

become friends. As friends, let Nebin and I help. We have a few days before the final rounds of the Duel Arcane."

Nebin gulped. Hennet shot him a raised eyebrow. The gnome nodded slowly, seeming to agree reluctantly. But Hennet knew that if the gnome really didn't want to help, nothing he did could convince Nebin otherwise.

Ember paused, then said with a glad voice, "We accept!"

She rewarded Hennet with another smile, and Hennet felt his eyes glaze over just a little.

Nebin fixed Kairoth, then Ember, with a penetrating look, and said, "All right, what's the next step? Back down into the catacombs, or do we spy out the Order to learn what Vobod's up to?"

Kairoth said, "Ember, Brek Gorunn, and I were just discussing that very question. I am loath to return to the catacombs so quickly. I believe we should enter the Order in secret, this very night. Perhaps we can learn what motivates Vobod and what foul force is aligned with him. Perhaps, as Brek Gorunn suggested, the cult of Nerull is active in all this, but I don't know how. I thought those cultists were all purged and gone. We must find out the truth, and the Order is the place to start."

Hennet said, "But, after all, maybe the old temple truly is the source of the evil. Those unquiet corpses were once in service to a death god, perhaps Nerull. And now that I think on it, what did you mean when you mumbled 'the Oath' as we rescued you?"

Kairoth looked uncertain.

"I vaguely recall it," he admitted, "but it eludes me now. It was something the death priest wanted me to repeat, but I wouldn't do it. All I know is that the words themselves were hideous, ghastly syllables."

Feeling as if he had scored a point, Hennet continued, "Then we should consider going back down there first."

Kairoth shook his head. "You may be right. But my instinct tells me that those unquiet dead are only a side effect. They are not the source of our troubles. They are only a symptom, one that must eventually be dealt with, too. If the catacombs in truth become our final destination, we shall only learn that by dealing first with Vobod."

Hennet couldn't argue with Kairoth's logic. Plus, he was tired.

He said, "If we're going tonight, we should rest. Nebin and I expended much of our arcane strength at the duel, and we need sleep. And, pardon me for saying so, you still look a little pale. It's only middle afternoon now. We could be rested and up again before the night is spent."

"Good," Kairoth said. "We will rouse three hours into the middle night. I will lead us into the Order via a secret route. The Order's traitors are not the only ones who know the ways of guile."

If the red masks or traitor monks somehow detected the intruders, Hennet argued, they could mount a stronger defense by concentrating in a single room, not by spreading into several rooms. As usual, Nebin disagreed and put forward his own theories. When Hennet and Ember left the room to see about getting more cots, Nebin approached the dwarf cleric. Brek Gorunn still sat at the room's one small table, sorting through a small collection of interesting items that included several closed leather cases of the kind traditionally used to protect spell scrolls. The dwarf was cataloging each item in the pile.

"Anything interesting?" asked the gnome.

"Yes," Brek replied. "These are the items we salvaged from the catacomb. As far as I can tell, they bear no taint of evil. We might find them useful. Some bear the imprint of spells arcane. Have a look. They'll do me little good—my power flows from Moradin."

The gnome was delighted. He shuffled through the documents. Many were nonmagical, or at least imprinted with a power he couldn't identify, and covered in an alphabet he couldn't decipher.

"I have no idea what these are."

He handed them back to Brek Gorunn, who rolled and stuffed the parchments into his satchel.

The gnome turned to the other documents. His fingers twitched in anticipation as he picked up the remaining two scrolls. One of his chief pleasures in life was the discovery of new spells that he could pen into his spellbook. He was a collector, and his collection was magic itself. He spread the scrolls wide open, gazing intently at the dancing glyphs. The inscriptions slowly ceased their movement, resolving into an arcane alphabet that was intimately familiar. The first was a spell that would allow one to fall from a great height without taking harm. That, Nebin thought, could be useful, in the right situation. He stuck that scroll in his belt, intending to inscribe it into his spellbook later.

The second spell would cause a creature to grow larger. Though it seemed disappointingly dull, he hated to waste any magical formula. Nebin read through the spell of enlargement again. It was fairly complex, and the more he studied it, the more he realized how much power was subtly woven into the spell. If he called on that power, he could be a giant! Nebin chuckled, imagining casting it on Hennet while he was sleeping, then watching his friend grow so large that he crushed his cot.

That gave Nebin an idea. He tucked the second scroll into his belt, also. Even if there wasn't enough time to scribe the complex spell into his book, he could cast it directly from the scroll. That would destroy the scroll, unfortunately, but it could well be worth it.

Brek, who still sat at the table, said, "You look happy. Has merciful Moradin blessed you?"

Nebin laughed. "Yes, I believe he has, Brek Gorunn. If Moradin wasn't called the Dwarffather, I might consider taking up your religion."

From across the room, Kairoth said, "Moradin is a worthy god, and we in the Enabled Hand have a long-standing relationship with the clerics of his order. You could do worse, Master Nebin."

"I suppose you're right," said the gnome, realizing he had a larger audience than just Brek. "So . . . Elder Kairoth, did you look through these other documents? They are not magical, but I can't read the writing on them. Perhaps they contain additional clues about what's befallen your Order."

"No, pass them over, I'll take a look."

Brek Gorunn, sighing, removed the lot from his satchel and walked them over to the elder. Despite his position, Kairoth's color already seemed better than when Nebin and Hennet returned from the duel.

Kairoth studied the manuscripts. He put aside several, saying, "I recognize the alphabet. It is Infernal, and creatures of Hell itself are said to use these characters in their terrible language."

"By Moradin's Hoary Axe!" exclaimed the dwarf.

Nebin's hair rose on the back of his neck. What were they involved in?

Kairoth looked up and said, "But the alphabet is also used by earthly creatures of ill will, seeking to emulate their masters. I suspect these were penned by a mortal cleric and not a demon. At least, I hope so. I can't read this script, it is too foul a study to take up, but this one is written in Common."

The page he held up was really only a fragment of parchment, its edges lost to time, its script nearly faded to illegibility.

Kairoth read from the parchment, " '. . . and so every soul to fall like chaff to the blade of the Reaper of Flesh. He that sits in eternal darkness waits at the end of every life, calling back to himself that which he has allowed, for a brief time, to frolic in the light. But the light is fleeting, and darkness eternal . . .' "

The dwarf glowered and said, "This 'Reaper of Flesh' claims too much. Moradin holds sway over the dwarves and their eternal destiny. This is lying propaganda."

Kairoth shrugged and said, "The text goes on in the same vein. This is a religious tract. Unless I misremember, the Reaper is one of Nerull's appellations. Another clue, but we already guessed Nerull might be involved. We need to find out who is attempting to revive Nerull worship, and why. Most importantly, we need to find out why the Order is involved at all."

"To gain a secret foothold?" ventured Nebin.

Kairoth's eyes widened slightly and he said, "It could be so. Who knows how far their reach already extends, with no one the wiser. We must put down this dark revival, and soon."

The dwarf clapped Kairoth on the shoulder. "Moradin willing, we shall," he said. "We are wise to their scheme, but they know nothing about us. Surely, the floors of the sacred Order groan under their sinful feet, but our footsteps will go unmarked. Tonight, we purge the evil from the halls of the Enabled Hand or die in the attempt. So say I, Brek Gorunn, Cleric of Moradin."

"Wake up, sleepyhead," said the voice.

Hennet opened one eye. Ember regarded the waking sorcerer with a smile. He returned her smile, groping for her hand, but she turned to wake the others. His hand fell back to his side.

She moved from cot to cot, waking everyone with a quick shake of the shoulder. She wasn't blind; she could see that the sorcerer was smitten with her, but his timing was not good. The loss of her chapter was too recent and weighed too heavily. Perhaps after the cult was dealt with, she could reach closure. Then she would consider the possibility of a deeper friendship with the sorcerer. But for now, she could not entertain distractions.

Though he is striking, she thought, *with those tattoos and his eastern mannerisms. . . .*

The streets of New Koratia at that late hour were still active. The five adventurers on their way to the Motherhouse of the Enabled Hand were just five more late revelers, among the many dozens still out late, seeking some last bit of entertainment before the dawn, only four hours away. They spoke little. The hard, bright stars looked down from on high, indifferent to the antics of the living.

Soon enough they stood in an alley near the Motherhouse. Ember felt a breath of danger on her neck and looked around cautiously. It reminded her of the night-darkened alley where she and Brek Gorunn had been ambushed. It wasn't a memory she was likely to lose. Judging by the way the dwarf clutched his warhammer, Ember concluded that Brek was recalling the same scene.

Kairoth rubbed his hands together as he approached one brick wall.

"A secret passage is here," he said, "but it is mostly forgotten. The younger elders do not know of it. It provided my escape when the Order was beset."

The older monk slowly walked along the wall, one hand trailing across the brick. The dim light from a street lantern threw his shadow along the wall before him.

"Ah, here it is."

A press, a twist, and a section of the wall whispered open.

Brek Gorunn noted in a professional tone, "Fine stonework."

Kairoth pressed a finger to his lips, motioning them to follow with his other hand. The elder stepped through the door into a narrow, dusty corridor. Ember followed him, then Brek and Hennet, and Nebin brought up the rear.

In the darkness of the passage, someone whispered, "Shall I summon light?" Ember recognized Hennet's voice.

The gruff voice of Brek Gorunn uttered a terse, "No." There were a few more seconds of darkness, then light blossomed from a lantern held by the dwarf. "Save your magic for the fighting, if it comes to it."

The narrow corridor ran parallel to the outer brick wall, then made a sudden turn, becoming even narrower, if possible. Ember felt sorry for the dwarf, who was barely able to squeeze along with his broad shoulders and mail overcoat. Kairoth led them to a small door.

The monk opened the door, revealing a small meditation cubicle. It held a single, flickering candle. Ember realized the door they had just opened into the cubicle was also secret.

She murmured back to the others, "This is a meditation chamber; we must be in the Hall of Meditation. Good news; we are close to the Elders' Sanctum."

Brek nodded, whispering, "The more of the Motherhouse we can bypass completely, the more likely we are to succeed."

"If we can avoid raising a general alarm, all the better. I do not want to fight innocent students," Kairoth agreed.

So saying, the older monk moved into the cubicle and opened the far door. Beyond was a broad hallway lit with golden lanterns, though all were burning on low wicks. Ember and the others followed, one after the other, passing out of the meditation cubicle, which was normally considered large enough for only a single student. Nebin followed Brek into the hallway, and Hennet followed after, closing the door with a tiny click.

Ember scanned the hallway, relieved to see that their entry was unmarked. Sometimes those who couldn't sleep visited the Hall of Meditation late at night to calm their thoughts.

Kairoth looked around and grimaced. "The Elders' Sanctum lies at the end of the hall."

They moved as a group in the direction the elder indicated. Ember recalled walking that very hall when she and Brek first visited the order two days before. A definite air of threat suffused the air, or at least she imagined so. A richly carved set of oak doors stood closed at the end of the hallway. The doors were framed in a matching oak lintel. The last time Ember and Brek passed that way, the doors were open.

Ember cocked her head. "Do you hear that?" Indeed, all could hear the mutterings of many voices in the next room, muted by the stout door. "It is some sort of gathering. I've never known the elders to meet so late."

Ember looked to Kairoth, and the elder shook his head.

"Any elders we see beyond this door are masters in the art of hand, fist, and foot, even if they've been somehow subverted. It would be foolish for any of you to try your strength against them. Leave them to me. Are you ready?"

Nebin brought his goggles down over his eyes and pulled a scroll from his belt. Hennet rubbed his hands together, while the dwarf smacked the head of his warhammer into his other palm.

Ember simply nodded and said, "It is time."

Kairoth pushed wide the door.

Two days before, Ember was heartened by the warm lights and fragrant oils of this chamber. Now, the ambiance of the reddish lights seemed to suggest only blood.

Four people sat in a circle at the center of the large room. All four wore red masks and chanted in atonal unison. At the center of the circle were two more figures. One was a woman half wrapped in gray strands of fabric, lying face up. She seemed drugged, unaware of her surroundings. Another red-masked figure hunched over her, tightening the woman's wrappings, winding the fabric around her slowly and ritually in time to the chanting. Ember recognized both. The woman being wrapped was Elder Cestra, the other, Elder Vobod! The walls of the room were hidden by silken screens.

Elder Kairoth spoke loudly. "Vobod, your betrayal of the Order ends here."

The chanting ceased as every masked face turned toward the intruders.

Vobod looked up, easily recognizable despite his red mask, and said, "Look here, my fellow adepts. We have more applicants who wish to take the Oath. Welcome them!"

The chanters scrambled to gain their feet. Elder Kairoth didn't give them the chance. With a yell, he leaped spectacularly over their heads and delivered a powerful spinning kick to Elder Vobod. Vobod deflected most of the force with the back of his hand, then counterattacked; he was a blur of flashing arms and legs. Normally, an exhibition fight between two elders was something Ember wouldn't miss. Now, she had to somehow deal with the other red-masked chanters. She hoped there were no elders hiding among them, or the battle was over before it began.

With a rush of feet, the red masks leaped to the attack, one after another.

Ember engaged the foremost, using careful *ho shin sul*, the self defense techniques of the Order. She was slightly dismayed when the man she faced used a similar, if not identical, technique. A stunning, round-house thunder slap to his neck penetrated his defense before he could counterattack. Ember spun past the collapsing man, looking for more adversaries.

Her breath caught when she saw robes cartwheeling past her and Brek's flank, directly toward Hennet. The sorcerer traced a pattern in the air, then reduced his assailant to a writhing heap on the floor with sizzling bolts of magic. Though the man fell, the momentum of his charge pushed the body to within a foot of the sorcerer.

Two more menaced Brek Gorunn, each attempting to distract the dwarf so that the other could attempt a killing blow. Before Ember could assist, Nebin rushed forward, one of his hands aglow with frigid lambency. When the gnome's hand brushed one of Brek's attackers, the supernatural charge stopped him cold. A heartbeat later, the dwarf dropped the other with a ringing blow from his warhammer.

Kairoth and Vobod continued sparring, two blurred forms moving too quickly to resolve. The dwarf howled his cry to battle, attacking Vobod from the rear. Before the dwarf's roar was fully formed, a foot lashed against his neck. The cry choked off and Brek collapsed, unmoving. Ember, on the dwarf's heels, stopped to check on him. He breathed, but his neck was badly crushed. Ember looked up, wondering if she should pull the dwarf away or help her mentor. No decision was necessary.

With the dwarf as a distraction, Elder Kairoth executed another spin kick. This time, Vobod had no defense. With the sound of crunching bone, Vobod joined Brek Gorunn on the floor. Kairoth stood as a pillar, unmoving, but his eyes danced.

It was then that a brutish, hollow voice echoed in the chamber. It said, "Elder Kairoth, remember your oath!"

Kairoth staggered as if punched, then stood unmoving again, but the flames in his eyes were doused.

"Who said that?" squealed Nebin.

Ember darted her gaze around, trying to ascertain the same thing. It hadn't been the last chanter. He cowered on the floor.

A shape burst through one of the screens surrounding the room, tearing the silk into flapping shreds. It was humanlike, yet bestial, half-again as big as a human. Its skin was muddy green.

Nebin squeaked, "An ogre! Or half-breed?"

The gnome's voice wavered with uncertainty. The ogre-like monstrosity laughed.

"Elder Kairoth," it intoned hollowly, "kill the woman! Then kill the rest!"

Kairoth grunted, his face working hard. Ember looked at her mentor, taking a step back. With a strangled grunt, he faced Ember.

He whispered, the muscles of his neck straining like wires, "Run!"

Ember nearly fell. Whatever had happened in the subterranean temple, they had not rescued Kairoth in time. It would have been clear to anyone that Kairoth's will was fighting the magical effect with supernatural effort. To Ember, who knew the mental disciplines behind the Order's training, the struggle playing out on Kairoth's face was a nightmare to behold. If Kairoth could not overcome it, she knew no one could. That would indeed be powerful and frightening magic—and the ogre somehow manipulated it. The monster had to be dealt with, and quickly. None of them would live long if Kairoth turned fully against them.

"Hennet, Nebin, kill that ogre *now!*" she screamed.

She wanted to say more, but Kairoth kicked at her. Another kick, two feints, and then a hammer blow so fast and hard it made the air ring. Ember fell back with each attack, knowing she couldn't fight her mentor. She barely dared to deflect his blows, afraid that even a glancing hit could shatter her arm or snap a wrist. She dodged and ducked, leaped and rolled, anything to stay away from those hands and feet that could strike like hot iron. If she could avoid getting crippled or knocked out, perhaps she could keep Kairoth occupied long enough for the others to eliminate the ogre that drove the monk to attack.

These were no thoughts in Ember's mind, only instinct. No time existed for thought. The notion had barely formed when a steely fist streaked past her whirling defense. Even as she was lifted from her feet and lost track of the room's orientation, she marveled at the elder's speed and power. How could a human do such feats?

She smashed backward through a silk screen and slammed into the solid wall behind. The force of the impact sent spiderweb cracks through the stone. Only when she slid down and collided with the floor did Ember realize she was upside down. Darkness's seductive veil tantalized her eyes.

Ember moaned, rolled onto all fours, and crawled forward. Blood dripped from the corner of her mouth, more streamed down her shoulder. She tried sitting up, pulling at the rough stones on the wall behind the screen for support, but her head swooned and up and down rushed together. Her back slapped the floor in a puff of dust. Lying there, she managed to turn her head so she could watch how the others fared without her.

Kairoth stood unmoving again, his hands squeezing into fists then relaxing, over and over. His face was beet red and sweat rolled across it to disappear into the knotted muscles of his neck. Ember looked for Hennet, then saw him facing the ogre. The sorcerer muttered a few syllables and gestured. A ghostly, disembodied hand appeared above and behind the ogre. The ogre didn't seem to see it—it was yelling something to Kairoth, but she couldn't hear over the thumping in her ears.

The ghostly hand, moving as Hennet's own hand moved, grabbed a loose drape of silk, one of the sheets torn by the ogre's entrance.

What's he up to? she wondered.

With a flip and a shake, the hand flicked the silk over the head of the ogre. The ogre roared and groped for the edge of the cloth. Ember saw Nebin skip forward. The gnome's hand was still charged with icy cold. He reached out and up, touching the creature in the middle of its chest. The ogre stiffened, its head wrapped in the silk.

It gasped, "Mistress Sosfane, help me! Nerull, preserve me."

Then it fell. Its heart was frozen.

Something occluded Ember's view. Kairoth! She flinched back as he reached toward her.

"Ember, a magical compulsion held me. I am so, so sorry. Please, let me help you."

He held her hand, and she allowed him to help her stand. Ember groaned. Once she was on her feet, her head cleared quickly.

With a hand on her mentor's shoulder, she said, "It was only your teaching, Kairoth, that allowed me to evade your attacks for as long as I did. And your last blow, I believe, would have killed anyone not trained by you."

Kairoth sighed and said, "A blackness fell over me. Something other than my own will directed my actions."

Ember nodded and vowed silently to keep one eye on the elder. His situation was a topic that required discussion, but it could wait.

Nebin remained where he stood before the unmoving ogre, breathing hard through his mouth. Ember presumed he was dazed or surprised at his own foolhardiness.

Hennet pulled a vial from his pouch and went to the dwarf's side. The sorcerer put the vial to the dwarf's lips, forcing him to drink. A gulp, a cough, and Brek Gorunn's eyes popped open.

Seeing Hennet, he asked, "We are the victors, then?"

Hennet nodded wearily.

Vobod and Cestra both lay unconscious. Neither showed any sign of coming around, but they continued to breathe shallowly. After a search of all the defeated cultists and their equipment, the group considered the fruits of their victory. They had collected several mundane rings and amulets bearing Nerull's sign, a few vials of magical liquid that Nebin promised to "keep safe" for later identification, and a single rolled parchment containing a message to Vobod. The message was inked in Common:

Dearest Vobod,
    Administer the Oath to Elder Cestra. Her unwitting cooperation has been useful, but the time has come to bring her

fully into the fold. Our secret is in danger of spilling out.
Kairoth has resurfaced. I blame you for leaving him to his own
devices in the Old Temple. He should have been brought to me,
in the Revived Temple, as I commanded. You will receive your
punishment in due course for this lapse. But for now, tend to
Cestra. Things come to a head. Nerull's umbral glory is about
to shine forth from the flaming pit. Let all fall before the
Reaper of Flesh!

—S.

" 'S,' eh?" wondered Nebin.

"Perhaps 'S' stands for Sosfane," said Ember. "When we spoke
with Elder Vobod earlier, he mentioned someone named Sosfane.
He claimed she had been slain, but it's obvious he lied about many
things. Assuming 'S' and Sosfane are one and the same, what does
she have against the Order of the Enabled Hand? I asked Vobod
that question earlier, but he wouldn't answer."

"It could be that she is simply exploiting a weakness to further
her cause," Hennet mused. "Maybe the Order of the Enabled
Hand is only involved because Vobod, or some other elder, proved
weak?"

"Hard to say," Kairoth responded. "We have few facts, and spec-
ulation won't lead us to the truth."

Nebin nudged Hennet in the ribs with a grin.

"Where is this 'Revived Temple' the note speaks of?" wondered
Ember.

Kairoth shook his head and said, "If anywhere, it is below the
city. The duke would never accept a temple to Nerull operating
openly on the streets."

Hennet asked, "Do you suppose it is near where we rescued
you, Elder Kairoth?"

"It may be, though this letter suggests that they are not near each other. Lucky for me, it seems," said the elder with unaccustomed irony.

"What is our next move? Despite all we have done here, this letter makes clear that we have not rooted out the source of the evil afflicting the order," Ember said, looking to Kairoth for direction.

"Find the Revived Temple," Kairoth replied. "Then we eliminate it, just as they attempted to eliminate us. We must fight or perish, that much is clear."

Ember considered. "I concur, except for one thing. I mean no offense, Elder Kairoth, but you have become vulnerable to them, and your vulnerability places all of us in great danger. You could be turned against us again, should you accompany us on our search for the Revived Temple. The same is true of Cestra, and potentially any other monk of the Enabled Hand. As far as I know, I am the only one who hasn't had contact with the Order before a few days ago. The task falls on me."

"Ember, you can count on me to help," declared Hennet.

"By the beard of my father, she can count on all of us, of course," agreed Brek Gorunn.

Nebin nodded. "Right. But lest we forget, tomorrow Hennet and I have one final obligation to fulfill in the coliseum."

Ember smiled. "Don't worry, wizard. It will take a day or longer to track down the whereabouts of this Revived Temple. Brek has other contacts in town, at the Temple of Moradin. Perhaps they can tell him where to start looking."

Ember turned to the dwarf, who said, "I will pay a visit to the Dwarffather's temple tomorrow morning, first thing. If there is any activity below the city, temple or not, my kindred here should know of it."

"Very well," concluded the elder. "I and Cestra will restore order in the Motherhouse as much as we are able. We will also question Vobod when he wakes—under strict guard, of course. Perhaps we can persuade him to tell us where the Revived Temple is located."

"Revived Temple of Nerull," Nebin pondered aloud. "I don't believe I like the sound of that."

It was good to be back in the coliseum. Screaming and cheering spectators crammed the stands. They "oohed" and "aahed" at flashy exhibition spells cast by the College of Wizardry staffers to entertain between events. The duel had gone on during Nebin and Hennet's absence, though not for novice casters. The intermediate, name, and grandmaster casters competed, and the stories from some of the individual duels were extraordinary. In fact, Nebin and Hennet arrived in time to watch the final round of the Grandmaster class.

Nebin sidled up to a judge and asked, "Who's dueling?"

Without moving her eyes away from the duel, the woman responded, "It's Incanus versus Ronassic. Incanus is a pyromancer from around here. Everyone knows he's started more fires than he's admitted to. Now, they say Ronassic is from a place so far away that miles can't be used as a measure—a fancy way of saying 'extraplanar,' I suppose."

Nebin nodded, suitably impressed. He turned his eyes to the duel, watching as Incanus hurled three balls of roaring fire at

Ronassic. The fury of his attack lapped out of the dueling area, starting secondary fires. Nebin and Hennet were pushed back as the ready crowd shuffled backward several feet.

Ronassic stood unharmed and apparently unconcerned. Incanus growled out an oath, then called burning magma like rain from the sky. The magma sent the crowd scuffling back even farther, but Ronassic only smiled as the fiery gobs of burning earth splattered down, always missing him. Ronassic screamed in apoplectic fury. A flurry of words poured from his mouth, and where he had been standing now stood a twenty-foot-tall creature of roaring flame!

Ronassic weathered the attack of the fiery creature without harm, still affecting a lackadaisical, waiting posture. Finally, he raised one eyebrow as if making a comment on Incanus' provincial ways. The crowd murmured loudly in response, and a cheer went up, "*Ronassic!*"

The mage shrugged and walked toward the hulking creature of fire. Incanus, suddenly realizing he might be on the wrong track with all the fire, shrank back to his normal size and form. Before he could do more than say, "Oh-oh," Ronassic reached out and touched the cringing wizard. As finger touched sleeve, a sphere of force enveloped Incanus like an eyelid closing. Then, as easily as a stone sinking in water, the sphere fell into the earth, leaving behind only a simple crater.

Silence reigned for seconds as Ronassic stood looking around as if unconcerned with his display of incredible power.

Hennet poked Nebin and whispered, "We have a lot to learn."

When Ronassic was declared the winner, the crowd cheered. Ronassic waved, accepting his accolades with easy grace.

"Wow. Have you ever seen magic wielded so well? I wish we could have seen the others," complained Nebin.

He and Hennet were jostled by the press of novices waiting

to begin their final round, now that the grandmaster competitions were complete. "Press" was the wrong word—there were only eight novice casters who qualified for the finals. Looking at that small group, Nebin realized how exceptional it was that he and Hennet both qualified.

Hennet interrupted his thoughts. "Nebin, had we stayed yesterday, Ember would have been without our help. Surely, doing good in the world and helping those in need is worth more than your entertainment?"

The gnome cocked his head toward his friend. "I want to watch the duel, you want to watch the monk. I don't see a big difference."

Hennet flushed, embarrassed. "There is a difference."

Nebin waited for the sorcerer to continue, but Hennet's gaze strayed to the stands. Ember was sitting somewhere out there—Hennet had asked her to attend, and wonder of wonders, she'd said yes. Nebin scanned the crowd, too, but couldn't locate her within the yelling throng.

Nebin suddenly felt a hand clasping his shoulder—a similar hand clasped Hennet's shoulder. It was Aganon, who had strolled up from behind them.

Aganon said, "Look at them! All those people in the stands, all of them ready to see who wins or loses today. Really, what they want to see is a little blood, unless I miss my mark. We shouldn't disappoint them, eh Nebin?"

Nebin shrugged and said, "I suppose if it comes down to it."

Hennet studied the hand on his shoulder. Nebin shrugged out of Aganon's clasp, wishing he'd been a little less friendly to the human when they first met. Something about Aganon didn't strike him as quite right. Nebin tried to put his finger on it, but all he could come up with was that the man's bravado seemed overshadowed by . . . insincerity.

" 'If it comes down to it?' " repeated Aganon. "The crowd demands a show, and I for one am up to that challenge. Those who win the Golden Wand are expected to possess a certain showmanship—a sense of entitlement. And I excel in both areas, as you may have noticed." Aganon chuckled.

"Well, may the best man win," replied the gnome. "Though you should know that I intend the Golden Wand for myself."

Aganon's usually jovial facade faded for an instant as he said, "Yes, let the best man win, Nebin, but a word to the wise: Don't hinder me, and things will continue to go well for you. I'm not someone you'd care to upset."

Nebin's witty response failed to find his mouth. Aganon's quick anger was like lightning out of a cloudless sky and just as disconcerting. The gnome frowned, understanding he'd just been threatened.

Aganon smiled, the threat wiped away as easily as a hostler wipes crumbs from a table. "But I'm sure it won't come to that. Good luck!"

He laughed jovially, and moved to stand closer to the edge of the arena, watching as another exhibition spell display wound down.

Nebin turned to Hennet and said, "Now, I call that downright odd. For a second, he seemed about to bite my head off. The next, he was as happy as a cat in a milk barn."

Hennet, who had watched the entire encounter, said, "He's a snake ready to shed its skin if ever I saw one. Watch him, I say."

Nebin said, "Don't worry. If luck is with us, he'll lose in the first round."

"If such comes to pass, then the gods indeed are looking out for us, Nebin," said the sorcerer.

Hennet suddenly cocked ear and said, "Listen! We're up. Luck to you, Nebin."

The crowd quieted slightly when the novice final rounds were announced. The first four rounds were called simultaneously. Nebin watched as Hennet was called to face a portly human man in too-tight-fitting orange robes, named Semeel Schniedly. Aganon squared off against a halfling woman in gray who had several short wands strapped to each forearm. Nebin hoped he wouldn't face her wands in the future, but hoped all the same that she would overcome Aganon. Two other mages faced each other, but Nebin didn't catch their names; he'd worry about that if he met one later. He had his own opponent to size up.

Nebin's competitor was a pale-skinned man wearing yellow pants, yellow boots, and a fine, yellow coat. His hat was likewise yellow, but a red feather was stuck in it. His white beard was neatly tied into many small braids on which arcane charms hung.

Fabulous Kuzon was the name the judges called. Nebin had to hand it to him—the human knew how to dress.

"Ready, Fab?" asked Nebin, using the diminutive of the man's name purposefully.

Fabulous Kuzon shot the gnome a sour look. Nearby, Nebin heard the judges for other rounds give the command to begin. Magical flares sparked over the floor of the coliseum—one nearly blinded the gnome. The roar of the crowd rumbled, and banners of all colors waved.

That was when their judge yelled, "Begin!"

The gnome, blinking the light out of his eyes, gestured and uttered words to a spell he considered an old friend. With it, he produced a freestanding pattern of pulsing, flowing, hypnotic lights. Nebin waved his hands, manipulating the colorful swirls to do his hypnotic bidding. He shot a glance at Kuzon, to see what effect his spell was having. If he was lucky, Fab was already staring and drooling like an idiot, but there was no such luck. Kuzon's eyes were closed.

The yellow-clad man finished his own spell and with eyes still closed, directed a beam of violet light from his fingertips toward Nebin. The gnome ducked, and the beam passed over his head with inches to spare. It struck a banner behind him. Both the banner and the beam winked out.

What's he throwing around? wondered Nebin.

The gnome continued swirling his hypnotic pattern in the air, but Fabulous Kuzon steadfastly refused to open his eyes. Worse, he began chanting and waving his hands again. Nebin hoped his foe wasn't preparing another purple zinger like the last one. It was time to improvise.

"Ugh, what did you do to me, Fab? I'm melting!" screamed Nebin.

"What?" gasped Kuzon, opening his eyes.

His gaze darted to the swirling pattern—and didn't dart away. His mouth gaped, his hands paused in their motions. The yellow mage's spell was ruined—Fabulous Kuzon was hypnotized!

The match was called in Nebin's favor. Those in the crowd who happened to be watching cheered, though a few booed. Nebin guessed that Fabulous Kuzon had fans—too bad for them.

The diminutive wizard walked back to the sidelines, his spirits ramping. That was his easiest match yet! He knew better than to expect another easy contest. He recognized dumb luck when he stepped in it. Still, if he could win the next round, the semifinal, he would advance to the final! His stomach was trying to climb up his throat. Apprehension would be his worst opponent, if he couldn't get it under control.

A dozen or more magical duels continued, leaking magic into the air. Most were not even novice-level duels. The name-level semifinals were being held concurrently. Fierce volleys of wizardry sparked everywhere, distracting his eye. Whose eyes wouldn't be snared by the sight of dozens of streaking meteorites impacting somewhere on the field, each burning like a tiny sun and sending sharp shadows fleeing away? Or the brief appearance of a summoned dire bear the size of an elephant? But where was Hennet? And Aganon? Nebin thought how pleasant it would be to see Aganon eating his hat.

A second novice duel was decided, that between the two mages whose names Nebin had missed. A woman named Felecia, with catlike ears, was declared the winner. Her competitor lay sprawled in enchanted slumber.

Not a second later, Aganon was declared the winner of his own duel. The answering roar of the crowd was strong. Aganon strutted, saluting the stands, but his competitor, the halfling woman, lay burned and bleeding, halfway out of the competitive circle. Two of her wands were broken on the ground. Attending clerics rushed the circle, curative potions at the ready. Nebin winced. He hoped that whoever Aganon faced next would prove the mage's better. Aganon's tactics were questionable, and the gnome couldn't help noticing that Aganon's satchel fairly bulged with scrolls.

Hennet's duel wore on. The dragon-tattooed sorcerer pelted orange-robed Semeel Schniedly with spheres of sorcerous light. Nebin had seen the sorcerer use that very power to great affect in the past, striking enemies like tiny hammers. But against Schniedly, Hennet's spell faded. A shield of glowing orange hung before Schniedly, moving as he moved. Each and every one of Hennet's missiles impacted on the shield harmlessly. Grinning widely, Schniedly cast a spell back at Hennet. The sorcerer stumbled under a rain of tiny, icy stones.

Nebin gravitated closer, yelling, "Get him, Hennet! He's a lousy poser, and a poor dresser."

Nebin heard other voices cheering Hennet's name in the stands. He looked up and finally saw Ember. She was standing and waving, and several other people stood around her. All called out Hennet's name.

But the situation didn't look good for Hennet. He weathered another torrent of icy stones, barely. He staggered and stumbled on the slickened ground. The sorcerer pulled a tattered parchment from his cloak. Nebin recognized it—his friend had carried that ragged scroll since their very first foray together. He held it in one shaking hand.

Nebin tried to recall the spell on the sheepskin, but only for a moment. Then it didn't matter. Hennet croaked out the mystic words, gesturing toward Schniedly, and nothing happened. That final effort was too much for him. Hennet collapsed, unconscious.

"Get up!" whispered Nebin.

But something was also wrong with Schniedly. A look of panic crossed the man's face as he looked down. A layer of greasy liquid flowed up from the ground beneath his feet, forming an inky layer around him. Hennet's spell was working after all! The man in the orange suit tried to hold still, but a breeze caught him. Frictionless, he skated right out of bounds.

The judge called, "The duel goes to Hennet Dragonborn!"

Despite lying unconscious, Hennet was still in bounds and his opponent was not. Nebin squawked happily, but his voice was lost in the screams of the boisterous crowd around Ember. They cheered again after an attending Peloran brother applied a vial of potent curative liquid to the sorcerer's lips. As Hennet stood, he waved up to the stands, even going so far as to blow a kiss to Ember.

"You're a bold one," laughed Nebin, but he also saw Ember laugh, apparently pleased with Hennet's antics.

Hennet ambled up to Nebin and said, "I knew that old scroll would come in handy."

The gnome clapped his friend on the back.

The novice competition was down to just four contestants: Hennet, Nebin, the strangely catlike Felicia, and Aganon. In only minutes the semifinal pair-ups were called. Hennet was matched against Felecia, and Nebin was paired with Aganon.

"Drat my luck!" Nebin swore, but not too loudly, because Aganon stood near. He didn't want the man to know he was afraid.

Hennet and Felicia walked out to begin their match, to the accompaniment of several loud, colorful conjurations. Nebin supposed they were designed to get the attention of the audience, but he didn't see any more. His mind was on Aganon. The gnome felt his heart sinking. This would be his toughest match.

They were led to a ring by an excited judge. Nebin and Aganon took their places as yet more colorful displays of wizardry drew the crowd's attention to their ring. The judges sensed this would be an exciting match, and they wanted the crowd to take notice.

The judge called out, "Nebin Raulnor, wizard, novice, faces off against Aganon, wizard, novice. You have three minutes to duel, and they begin . . . *now!*"

The gnome, unsure of what tactic to use, fell back on his favorite—the illusory flaming ball, ten feet across. He called the sphere above Aganon and let rivulets of fire cover the man. Aganon was unperturbed for the few seconds he was visible before the flames hid him. The gnome felt emboldened now that he couldn't see Aganon. Nebin took the opportunity to sidle to the left. He might gain a small edge if Aganon didn't know exactly where he stood.

Without his volition, the flaming ball dispersed—always a bad sign, Nebin thought. A green glow surrounded the suddenly revealed Aganon. The man gestured at the gnome. A wave of green fluid swept up from nowhere, surging around Nebin's feet. He shrieked and tried to jump away, but it was as if he were caught in the undertow of an ocean wave. Where the liquid touched him, pain flared. With cruel slowness, the wave inexorably bore the screaming gnome across and out of the ring.

Nebin had lost.

Hennet worried. Felecia dodged two of his sorcerous missiles with uncanny quickness. No one had ever done that before. In fact, he was pretty sure it was impossible, and the knowledge only made the feat that much more impressive. He was close to exhaustion and none of his spells had found their mark. Even worse, Ember was watching and would see him defeated.

Felecia laughed. "Might as well give up, sorcerer. You know I'm only toying with you."

The woman had furred ears, large green eyes, and clawed hands. Hennet guessed her feet were also clawed, but he didn't bother to look. Mentally he scrambled for a new strategy, but his mind was a winter plain, bereft of life.

Stalling for time, he muttered, "You're not half as quick or gorgeous as you imagine, lady."

Felecia's eyes came near to popping from her head as she snarled, "You have no right to judge me, human!"

"Maybe not," Hennet shot back, "but I know beauty when I see it, and you're not it—mongrel!"

He tossed in that last word on a hunch, sensing he was on to something. In other circumstances, Hennet would have found Felecia enticingly exotic. Now he had to use every available weapon, including attacks on her ego and self esteem.

Felecia bristled, then screamed, "I'll see you in Hell, human!"

A rain of claws descended on Hennet, who gasped, stumbling back. His feet caught on the rocks marking the boundary of the duel. As quick as that he fell out. And Felecia was on him, roaring.

She's going to kill me! Hennet realized, trying to protect his eyes from the flashing claws. He could hear the judges yelling, the crowd screaming. He kicked out, but Felecia dodged and cut his cheek to the bone with a razor-sharp swipe. Blood gushed across Hennet's eyes, blinding him. More searing cuts lacerated him. All he could do was crawl away from the fangs and claws.

Air swooshed, and someone gasped—Felecia. She was off him. Hands helped him to his feet. A few of them belonged to Peloran brothers, apparently. The pain drained away, and Hennet's eyes cleared of blood. Gashes on his hands and arms closed as he watched. He looked up, searching for Felecia. She stood amid another group of judges. A net of silvery light held her immobile, though she continued struggling and glaring at him.

One of the judges conferred with another, then turned and yelled, "The novice Felecia is disqualified! The win goes to Hennet Dragonborn!"

What a world, Hennet thought as the crowd cheered. He was going to the final round!

Though physically mended, Hennet was tired. He felt he'd be lucky to dredge up the strength to cast even one more spell, let alone the three or four he would need to put up a real fight in the final round.

He looked around, up into the loud, surging stands. Ember was still there, waving. He gave her a thumbs-up sign, despite his doubts. She smiled back. Her smile was like ambrosia. She had seen him win twice against difficult odds. Knowing she was there had helped him in those matches. How much better would it be if she saw him win the Golden Wand? Perhaps she'd give him a victory kiss.

How much better would that be than winning the Golden Wand?

Hennet didn't know whether he could win against Aganon. He did know, however, that he couldn't back down, he couldn't even do less than his very best. Ember might understand if he lost, but not if he gave up. During the past few days, she replaced the wand as the prize he sought. Ember was the goal.

A tap on his shoulder brought Hennet around. It was Nebin. If Hennet hadn't known already, he'd have guessed the gnome was out from the way his goggles perched askew on his head.

"I'm sorry, Nebin," Hennet consoled. "I half expected us to face each other in the final."

Nebin waved away his concern and said, "Don't worry about it. Look at you! I never really thought I'd get as far as I did, and here you are a step from the Golden Wand, worrying about me. You'd better concentrate on Aganon. He's a beast." The gnome pointed.

There Aganon stood, grinning like a demon with his eyes closed. His mouth moved as if he spoke to someone, but no one stood nearby. He clasped his hands as if praying; Hennet realized he was offering obeisance or thanks to some god, and wondered which. Hennet's eyes were drawn to Aganon's scroll-stuffed satchel.

"He must have friends willing to contribute to the cause. I hope those scrolls are just messages wishing good luck. If they're all spells . . . well, I'm pretty tired."

Nebin snapped his fingers and said, "I almost forgot! Here, take this." The gnome produced a scroll tube. "This is a spell we retrieved from the catacombs. It's not a sure-fire winner, but it's better than nothing."

Hennet examined the scroll, sealed with wax stamped with the gnome's personal symbol. To the gnome, every penned scroll was precious. Hennet realized that Nebin was making a real sacrifice, though he played it down.

"Thank you, Nebin. I appreciate your friendship, you know," said Hennet.

"Ah, you'd do the same in my boots. Now listen, here's what you need to do . . ."

The gnome leaned close. Hennet bent over, and Nebin whispered his plan, such as it was, into the sorcerer's ear. Hennet grinned on hearing it. He wondered about the wizard sometimes.

A judge wearing the badge of the Floating Tower summoned Hennet and Aganon to the central ring. Because this was the final round of the novice competition, the other matches paused. The whole stadium focused on Hennet and Aganon. Hennet steeled himself. He had to ignore the distracting roar of the coliseum and approach the bout like any other. Despite his resolve, he realized the duel's outcome was all that stood between him and the Golden Wand—and, possibly, Ember.

He stared at Aganon with hard eyes, and the man glared back undaunted. Aganon held one hand half raised, ready to cast at the drop of a copper. Hennet raised a hand in the same manner, though he had no spell clearly in mind.

And so it began.

His tried-and-true barrage of enchanted missiles was unlikely to win him the match. Hennet didn't know if he had the resources to call even one. He had Nebin's scroll, but it wouldn't work immediately, not while Aganon remained where he stood. Hennet had to get the man to move. No spell he'd ever learned could do that.

That left one option. Hennet had to reach for magic he'd never before cast. During his daily meditations, hints of power whispered from the caves of his subconscious. What was the meaning in those whispers? Something was there. . . .

An arrow of liquid acid stabbed into his forearm. Hennet yelled as the glob bubbled and burned on his arm, wispy tendrils of smoke winding up from a point of agony.

"You make this too easy!" taunted Aganon. "Continue standing still, and save yourself some grief."

The pain from the acid was intense, like a drill . . . like a goad . . . or better yet, like a torch of brilliant flame. Was it a torch Hennet could use? He imagined that torch probing the edges of his conscious mind, casting a dimly flickering illumination into the whispery shadows where subconscious revelations hid. And there he found something. It was only a strand of power, maybe the tail of a racial memory of spellcasting, but Hennet saw himself grasping it, grappling with it, pulling it into the full light of consciousness. It was none of the things he'd imagined, and it was all of them and more. It was one more piece of the knowledge that lay latent within him since his birth, a legacy shared through countless ages by every sorcerer, thanks to imperceptible traces of dragon blood running in their veins.

Hennet uttered a string of syllables new to his lips and disappeared.

Aganon paused. He looked around the ring, then at the judge, who merely shrugged.

Aganon frowned and said, "Hiding isn't going to help, you know. There is a time limit. All I have to do is stand here, and I win."

Hennet wasn't sure the spell had worked until Aganon spoke. He looked down, exulting to see himself only as a vague, ghostly outline. No one else could see even that much. This was a moment of discovery to savor, but there was no time. As Aganon pointed out, invisibility alone would not win the match. Meanwhile, the acid in his forearm continued burning, weakening him slowly. He couldn't risk brushing it off for fear of spreading the caustic mess and making the injury and the pain worse.

He crept toward Aganon, aware that invisibility would neither conceal his footprints in the gravel nor cover the sound of grinding pebbles. His opponent stood closer to the center of the ring than the edge. Hennet wanted Aganon near the edge.

Hennet also knew, through his subconscious, that casting a spell at Aganon would dispel his own invisibility. The simplest solutions are often the best, he reminded himself. Moving as slowly as he dared under the match's time limit, Hennet stole to within a foot of Aganon, who stood unmoving, listening. When Hennet was just beyond arm's reach from Aganon, he lunged forward and clapped his hands, creating a mighty *thwack!* inches from Aganon's ear.

The wizard shrieked and scuttled backward. In fact, he tripped and almost—*almost*—fell right out of the ring. That would have been too easy, thought Hennet as he carefully unrolled the scroll Nebin had given him.

Aganon's features resumed their stoic cast. "Crude, and sad, too," he chided. "A magical strategy suited for children, perhaps. You make a mockery of the Duel Arcane. Show yourself. Is this a contest of magic, or buffoonery? Ah, there you are!"

Hennet faded back into view. In one hand he held Nebin's scroll. As he finished his quiet incantation, the inked arcane syllables faded from view, indicating that the magic stored in the parchment was expended. There was no obvious effect.

There was no shortage of excitement near Aganon, however. Roaring flames fanned from his outstretched fingers. They washed up against the sorcerer and kindled Nebin's scroll. Hennet dropped the smoking parchment and backed away, avoiding most of the spray of flames. Aganon followed, flames still spewing from his splayed fingers, in an attempt to force Hennet out the other side of the circle. Hennet knew that if his gambit didn't pay off soon, he would have to either step out of the ring or be burned alive.

Aganon looked around, a confused expression on his face.

"Why is everyone shrinking?" he muttered. "Why is the ring shrinking?"

Aganon looked at the judge, but she was shrinking, too. Her voice sounded small when she called out, "The final round is over. The win goes to the sorcerer, Hennet Dragonborn. He is the victor, and has rightful claim to the Golden Wand! Hail the sorcerer!"

The stands erupted in wild cheering and stomping. Sympathetic displays of minor illusion popped across the field, created by fellow wizards as congratulations to the victor.

Nebin ran up to his friend as Hennet patted out smoldering bits of leather.

"You used it! You followed the plan!" The gnome laughed happily.

The too-large Aganon glowered. He stood over ten feet tall and he was puzzled. How had he lost? Only when he twisted around did he see the reason. The spell of magical enlargement made him grow so much that he no longer stood entirely in the ring. His giant-size left foot had slid out of the ring. It was still mostly inside the painted ring, and yet it had undeniably broken the circle, placing him out of bounds.

The man's eyes glinted with a greenish light. A terrible anger moved there.

He thundered, "Do not think that I'll suffer defeat through so cheap a trick. It's only a matter of time before my friends and I take charge of things around here. We'll see who gets the Golden Wand!"

The judge, accustomed to sore losers, waved Aganon away. He thumped off, his enormous boots making wide tracks on the floor of the coliseum. That was when the cheering started in earnest.

At the award ceremony later that day, Nebin watched proudly, if a little enviously, as the Golden Wand was conferred on Hennet. The sorcerer stood on a small riser in the middle of the coliseum, beneath the shadow of the Floating Tower. To the accompaniment of a salute by the gathered college wizards, an aged mage with a gray-streaked beard presented Hennet with his trophy. It was smooth, slender, and golden-hued.

The wand shone with its own light, even in the full light of day.

"With the Golden Wand," declared the mage, "you can invoke the very weapons of your enemies and turn their magical power against them! Use it wisely. You are its keeper for now."

The wand glowed like sun-fired amber.

Hennet raised the wand above his head and shouted, "I thank the College of Wizardry for hosting the Duel Arcane. I thank all of you who have come to watch the wonders of wizardry and sorcerery displayed here. But most of all, I want to thank the unexcelled wizard Nebin Raulnor, with whom I shall share this award. I couldn't have done it without his help."

Nebin swallowed. The crowd cheered more wildly than before—Nebin had been the favorite of a very vocal gnomish contingent. He smiled back at his friend the sorcerer.

After the festivities, which included a special feast held by the college for the winners (and their closest friends) in all the categories, Hennet, Nebin, and Ember returned to the Cuttle-stone. Ember realized that her hearty congratulatory hug was the first overt sign she'd given the sorcerer that he was capable of winning her affection.

What effect might that have on him? she wondered.

Hennet, feeling gregarious and generous after his win, picked up the dinner tab in the common room. Thankfully, Brek Gorunn was not back from his fact-finding visit to the local temple of Moradin. Ember knew to beware the dwarf at table— his stomach was voluminous, and he would gladly take advantage of a free meal. When Brek Gorunn finally did appear, Hennet paid for the dwarf's meal all the same. The others had long since finished their meals. The menu was honey-braised duck slow roasted over cherry-wood embers.

When the dwarf finally sighed and pushed his plate away, he said, "I learned a few things at the dwarven temple today."

Ember sighed. She'd spent most of the day in a jovial and carefree mood, losing herself in watching the Duel Arcane. It was a nice break, but with the dwarf's words, she recalled her duty. It was time to get back to the matter at hand.

Ember asked the question on everyone's mind. "What of the revived temple of Nerull?" The words chilled the table.

The dwarf produced a leather case from his knapsack. Inside was a half-charred parchment—Ember realized it was a map. The dwarf laid it flat on the table, pinning down a curling edge with a handy tankard. Much of it was ruined by burn marks, but some lines remained visible, including a central area with many corridors leading outward.

"This map was made by a cleric of Moradin four hundred and sixty years ago, when the old temple of Nerull was discovered, and destroyed. Now, it's all history. This is the only document the clerics could unearth. The map reveals how the old sewers connect to the far older catacombs." The dwarf pointed to the nexus and said, "Here's where we found Kairoth."

"Catacombs? Are they part of the ancient city?" asked Nebin.

"Yes, pre-Koratia. Here before even the first wave of Nerull-worshipers appeared, but well suited to their needs. Anyway, the old temple of Nerull was based in the very center of the catacombs. The Father Superior at Moradin's Temple, who I spoke with at length today, warned that if Nerull's temple is revived, it likely lies where the old temple once hid—at the heart of the oldest catacombs."

All were silent, remembering their last trip to the mere edge of that lightless maze below New Koratia.

"Then, that is where we must go," said Hennet. Brek Gorunn nodded. Nebin put his head in his hands, sighing. Ember let Hennet have a brilliant smile.

"We should go soon," agreed Brek Gorunn.

"Soon!?" squalled Nebin. "Let's think about this. It would be so nice to simply relax. Let's say we order another round of wine? You can have ale, Brek, if wine doesn't suit you. No need to send us all off to the dungeons."

The dwarf chuckled, "Soon, not in ten minutes, Nebin. I learned a few more things about the catacombs today in Moradin's temple library. We need to make a few preparations, based on what I learned there, and I will have that mug of ale."

"Yes, let's purchase supplies at first light tomorrow," Ember concurred. "I'd like to head into the catacombs no later than noon."

Hennet pulled out his trophy from the Duel Arcane, inspected it, and said, "I'm eager to see if the Golden Wand's power will serve me. I'd like to see if it really can cage magical attacks thrown against me and return them back upon my attacker. What better test than in Nerull's catacombs?"

Nebin said, "How about not going into the catacombs and trying out the power right here in the Cuttlestone? Safer, I'd guess. I can fling a petty bolt at you."

"No, my friend, the wand's power is not unlimited. Better to use it only at need. I'd rather not squander it."

"Nebin, if you feel that a trip into the catacombs is not for you . . ." began Ember.

"Hold on, don't say it. Of course I'm coming with you. I'm just on the side of caution, that's all," said the gnome. "If not me, who will be the voice of reason?"

Hennet opened his eyes in mock surprise. "If not you? Let me recall to your mind a foray you and I shared last year. It was high summer—do you remember? We were summoned by the alchemist of Whitemore. You pulled that red lever in his laboratory. Oh, you recall that, I see! And do you remember what we went through because of that?"

Nebin interrupted Hennet. "Yes, yes, no need to sift through the whole incident."

Ember's and Brek's expressions indicated they actually wouldn't mind hearing the story, but Nebin continued speaking. "Anyway, we learn from our mistakes."

"I'm glad," said Ember. And she really was. The gnome was competent, even though he enjoyed playing the clown.

Nebin turned back to the dwarf and said, "And you're sure there is no other entry into the revived temple except through the catacombs?"

"Of course there is! But, we're sneaking in. We have a map of the ancient entrance. Presumably, the red masks enter and leave using some entrance closer to the surface. Our way is longer, more dangerous, but should ultimately give us the element of surprise."

Nebin nodded, apparently satisfied.

Ember finished her drink, wondering about the red lever Nebin had pulled. It could wait, but she would like to hear that story someday.

She said, "Wonderful. Tonight we relax. In the morning we prepare for our expedition against the cult of the death god."

At dawn, after an early breakfast, the four companions headed to the market quarter.

Shops could be found pretty much anywhere in the city, but they were concentrated in the market quarter. More importantly, the market quarter was home of the Wizard's Hoard. It dealt strictly in magic and had a first-rate reputation.

Like the Floating Tower, the Hoard was run by the College of Wizardry, though it didn't float. It was a rambling building of luminescent stone resembling blocks of pearl. The main structure was covered by a dome that glittered even in moonlight. Inside, thousands of arcane items could be bought and sold for a fair price.

The group entered through a wide portico and found themselves in a broad, covered bazaar. The ceiling, the interior of the vast dome, sparkled with stars as convincing as the night sky. Below, tents and carts crowded together at the center of the open area. These belonged to the hedge wizards and witches who rented space, selling minor charms and ointments from their wagons. The "good stuff" was to be found along the broad, curving walls, where permanent shop fronts were situated and run directly by the College of Wizardry. No-nonsense advertising hung above many of the shops, scribed in Draconic and other magical languages: Potions, Wands, Staves, Impenetrable Armors, Enchanted Blades, and more.

They stood gazing in wonder. None had ever been to the Wizard's Hoard before. It was a little overwhelming.

First, the group sold the trinkets, documents, and minor items retrieved when they rescued Kairoth. No buyer asked intrusive questions. Everyone purchased a few vials of magical curative. They knew it would be foolhardy to rely solely on Brek Gorunn to save them all from injuries.

Nebin bought some spare, spell-grade parchment.

Ember found a shop called Ellen's Elixirs and Charms. The shop proprietor was a withered, human woman who wore dozens of charms on strands around her neck. Though she hawked many potential wonders, in the end, Ember bought a potion advertised to "make a hero" of the imbiber.

After purchasing a single curative, the dwarf made a beeline for the shop along the round called Smite Plus. Inside, a cornucopia of oils, charms, and scribed spells were available, each offering a temporary enhancement to a weapon. Brek used nearly his last gold imperial to purchase a magical oil that would briefly empower his warhammer. He grinned as he walked out. It was good to serve Moradin!

Hennet bought nothing besides curative vials. He had the Golden Wand, after all. Its powers would be a great help. A few people in the dome even recognized him from the Duel Arcane and congratulated him on his victory.

They met again near the entrance. It was time to move on. After leaving the Hoard they visited a few other shops—Hennet needed crossbow bolts, Ember desired a new pair of gloves, Brek wanted rope, and Nebin pointed out that they could be in the catacombs for quite some time—they had better purchase provisions enough to last for two or three days.

Finally all the supplies were bought, inventoried, and stowed. Each wore a small pack, a pouch, and a satchel. It was time to descend into the lightless halls beneath the city. That was adventure enough on its own, but they knew that getting through the catacombs was only half the challenge. Finding and dealing with the revived temple of Nerull in the heart of the catacombs was their true task.

"There it is," said Ember, pointing at the rune-inscribed double door.

The sewers were behind them, the catacombs lay ahead. One of the stone doors remained open, as they'd left it. Inside, the chamber appeared unchanged. The pit trap gaped wide, opening onto a fall Ember remembered well.

Brek pushed into the room. Ember kept her eye on the far opening while Brek checked the pit.

"Seems clear," shrugged the dwarf. "Let's go."

With the dwarf ahead and Ember right behind, they entered the narrow, urn-lined corridor. As before, Hennet and Nebin brought up the rear. They avoided disturbing the urns, for fear they still held the remains of people long dead. Brek's lantern provided flickering and uncertain light, sending shadows chasing up and down the cemetery hallway.

The next chamber was also quiet. This is the room where we rescued Kairoth, reflected Ember. The room was circular, domed, and connected to six hallways. Each opening was shadowed with threat. During their last visit, greenish ghoul-light had lit the scene. Ember silently thanked providence that that foul radiance was gone, not to mention the animate, spellcasting corpse. Brek walked forward with his light and examined the floor around the altar.

He looked up and declared, "The mummy carcass is gone. Or it removed itself. Either way, something has been here since us."

"If you're suggesting we stay on our guard, don't worry," responded Hennet. "We are."

Brek grinned through his beard.

Hennet continued, "Which way does your map show now?"

Ember moved next to the dwarf as he set down his warhammer and lamp and pulled out the charred map. It indicated that of the six passages connected to this chamber, only one was marked—with a symbol of a skull and scythe.

Brek pointed at the corresponding passage across the room and said, "That way."

"How much farther to the temple?" asked Nebin.

The dwarf shook his head. "The map is only a fragment. If it ever had a scale, it's gone now. Pointing us down this corridor is the limit of its usefulness. I'll lead."

The dwarf held forth the lamp and plunged into the corridor. Ember walked to his right, and she heard Hennet and Nebin follow.

Like the last corridor, this one, too, was lined with elaborate urns. Unfamiliar glyphs on the sides of the urns winked below their ages-old blankets of dust. No one wanted to look at them too closely for fear of disturbing their contents. Almost immediately, the passage angled downward. After walking a long distance on the steep grade, the lantern revealed a mist in the air. The farther they pressed forward, the thicker the haze. Soon, it was a true fog. It smelled faintly of dank copper, or blood. Brek Gorunn's light was a glowing spot of blue in the darkness.

Ember put her hand on the dwarf's shoulder and murmured, "Slow down a bit. The mist could hide anything."

The dwarf grunted, but slowed. Ember thought all their footfalls sounded muffled, as if sound were strangled by the mist.

Eventually the grade leveled off and the passage issued into a room whose edges were obscured in fog. The vapors were acrid in Ember's mouth and nose and made her eyes water. Brek stopped short of entering, and she stopped with him.

Looking back, she said, "Stay close. It's impossible to say how big this room is, with the mist, and we don't want to lose anyone. We're going to follow the right-hand wall around the room. Keep your hand on the wall and you won't get lost. We'll follow it right around until we've come back to this entrance. That way, we won't miss any exits in this damnable fog."

Brek grunted his approval, and they moved out. The fog was thicker than ever.

The trip around the chamber proved a journey of only a minute, and they were moving cautiously. A single sealed exit opposite the entry was found during their circuit. A face, its mouth gaping wide, was carved in relief into the stone above the exit. Fell vapors issued from its mouth, constantly replenishing the haze in the chamber and the corridor leading to it.

"What sorcery is this?" wondered Ember, leaning close.

"Better ask, 'what wizardry,' " said Nebin.

Ember rolled her eyes, though she knew no one could see her.

Nebin continued, "I expect it is a relic of the ancient city. It's said that the ancient city housed a race of wizards. Well, best to fight wizardry with the same."

Ember saw Nebin melt out of the mist as he moved to stand next to her and the face. She couldn't decide what race the carving portrayed, if it was intended to portray any. Nebin frowned, then fumbled in his pockets. He pulled a kerchief from his coat, considered it for a moment, then handed it to Ember and instructed her to stuff it into the stone mouth. The spewing vapor ceased.

"A finer application of wizardry I've never seen," noted Hennet. "Perhaps with your next spell you can open the door?"

Nebin chuckled. He reached for the door ring and pulled. The door didn't budge, but a stony cough issued from the carved face. The kerchief popped from the mouth, propelled by a puff of greenish gas.

"Uh . . ." stammered the gnome, stumbling backward.

Ember grabbed Nebin around the waist and hauled him toward the entrance. Hennet followed, nearly as quickly. Brek Gorunn appeared a few moments later.

The dwarf sneezed and coughed a few times and said, "I got a whiff of it. Nasty. Poisonous, I expect. Best stay away until it clears."

"If it does," Nebin said darkly.

"It's an old trap," said the dwarf, "and spent, now that we've set it off. I'm sure the poison is weakened from the ages. Otherwise we would be short one gnome."

Nebin darted a look back into the hazy room. Ember could see the curl of greenish mist slowly expanding and diluting into the fog. Nebin shivered.

When Brek Gorunn decided all was clear, they cautiously returned to the door. As the dwarf said, there was no hint of the green gas. Better yet, the blue haze was lifting. The carved face seemed completely quiescent, as if some final bit of élan was now absent. Nebin gave it a tentative tap. Everyone breathed easier after a few seconds of no response.

This time, Ember and Brek tried the door together while Nebin hung back. The door still held fast.

"Put your shoulder into it, Ember," Brek Gorunn advised uselessly.

The tendons in her legs and back trembled, then with a *snap!* the door burst open.

Beyond, the lantern revealed a mist-free room. A mosaic of dark tile covered the floor and walls, though many tiles were cracked and broken. The faintest glitter of light edged the tiles, giving them a greenish tinge. Ember was pretty sure it wasn't a reflection cast by the lantern—it was a fell light all their own. Apart from the suspicious glow and scattered, broken tiles, the room was empty. Opposite their doorway stood a single, dark aperture. Bold runes were inscribed all around it.

Seeing the runes, Nebin tried to squeeze past the dwarf and enter the room. Brek Gorunn held him back.

"Hold on! Don't be foolish. Where there is one trap, there can be two, or more."

"I don't like the look of those tiles," Hennet concurred. "They have a cursed light about them, or I'm no mage."

Nebin seemed to restrain a comeback. Ember supposed it was because Hennet clutched the Golden Wand, proof positive that he knew a thing or two about magic.

Experimentally, Brek Gorunn closed the lantern's cover. A pale, green glow suffused the room, outlining each tile. Wordlessly he uncovered the lantern again.

"But we must go forward. W-we have no other route," sputtered Nebin.

Brek Gorunn paused on the threshold and squinted toward the far hallway.

"You can just read the runes from here," he said. "It looks to me like an archaic variant of the common tongue."

Nebin moved to stand next to Brek, his eyes narrowed in concentration.

The gnome said, "They state, 'Pass and Prosper if Ye be Reverent. Pass and Perish if Ye Profane Nerull.'"

Brek Gorunn spat. "How can you profane the blasphemous?"

Nebin shrugged.

Ember edged forward. She knew that of them all, she was the swiftest and most capable of escaping a purely mechanical trap, if indeed the tiles represented danger. The choice was hers to make. She entered the chamber, walking lightly, and passed unhindered across the tiled floor, right up to the rune-scribed archway. She looked back, allowing a smile to touch her lips.

"Seems safe enough."

Hennet let out a breath. He and the others entered without mishap, until they all stood by the archway. The corridor was visible beyond. Except for the ominous runes, nothing would have checked their passage into the innocuous walkway.

"Brek Gorunn asked a good question," mused Hennet. "Its counterpoint would be how do you revere a god of death?"

"I don't want to guess," said Ember.

The dwarf said, "I'll guess. Even without holy indoctrination, I could tell you that the act of murder is a reverent deed to this unholy deity of death." The dwarf spat once more.

"We're not going to kill someone just to get past the archway," exclaimed Ember.

She was prepared to sacrifice a lot, but not an innocent life.

Hennet nodded. "There has to be another way to the temple. How are all the cultists getting in and out?"

Brek shook his head. "If we wanted to come in the front door, we wouldn't be here in the first place."

"I have an idea," said Nebin, still studying the runes. He pulled a small dagger from his belt and looked at the others. "A violent death, of the sort we can assume this nasty death god prefers, produces blood. Maybe a drop would do as well as a bucket."

Nebin winced as he pricked a finger with his dagger. Blood beaded on his fingertip. The gnome flicked the drop, painting a copper-size portion on the glowing tiles red. The blood trembled, then was sucked into the stone, leaving not a trace.

The glimmer in the tiles faded. Something clicked, muffled by the walls. All was quiet once more.

"Well, I've either deactivated, or activated something. Who wants to go first?" asked Nebin.

Ember advanced, ready to jump back at the first sign of trouble. Again, she came to no harm. She motioned the others to follow, but not before giving the gnome a grateful look.

"You are wise beyond your size, Nebin."

The gnome nodded, accepting the compliment as his due. She shrugged and turned back to face front. Ember enjoyed giving the wizard compliments, if only to see him preen after each one.

They passed down the corridor, and the trap, if any, failed to materialize. On they traveled, descending farther as they went. The subterranean dark weighed on Ember. She sensed a similar depression in Hennet and Nebin, but not Brek Gorunn. She supposed the dwarf preferred the bosom of the earth to the open skies.

Soon Ember noticed that the stone walls of the passage were cracked. Seeping moisture widened some of the cracks over the years, forming gaping holes. They passed skull-carved balusters, looming in the swaying lantern's light. Their footsteps echoed as they walked, leaping ahead, then following behind. Again the corridor emptied into a chamber, much larger than the others. Shapes were revealed in the vast room; pale domes, biers, and carved sarcophagi with images of men long dead. Ember couldn't begin to estimate the size of the room, but the absolute stillness of the air and the hollow echoes from their small movements revealed that it was at least several hundred feet wide, if not more.

"This doesn't seem a particularly safe route," quavered Nebin. "Those are sarcophagi. You know, with dead people in them."

His words echoed with ominous portent. Quiet followed.

Ember realized the gnome was right. This was a sort of mausoleum. And it was old, probably older than any structure she had ever been inside.

She said, "Stay alert. I expect that those who have lain here so long have no more interest in the living, if they ever did."

Even as she spoke words of confidence, she debated internally. Stories and her own experience told her that it was always wise to expect to find undead prowling near tombs, even those considered safe.

Brek Gorunn motioned them ahead. The dwarf gripped his warhammer.

They passed into the chamber between tables and buildings carved from marble. The darkness was complete, sealing them inside the circle of Brek's light. They passed the ominous mouths of tombs carved with faces, bodies, skulls, and darker symbols. Maybe the old cult of Nerull once claimed the spaces beneath New Koratia, but Ember could see the tombs here were far older than a few hundred years, older than the founding of the city, stretching into the past even beyond the knowledge of the cultists who briefly claimed it.

The strains of a flute playing alone in the distance stopped Ember. The notes were placid and deep, as if a dirge.

"Do you hear that?" she asked.

Everyone stopped, straining their ears, but the ghost-music was silent.

"I think I heard it, for a second," said Hennet. "Pipes, maybe, or a fife?"

"It reminded me of a flute," said Ember.

Brek said, "I heard it, and did not like it, whatever its source. Best we press ahead swiftly, lest we meet the musician."

Passing deeper into the vast underground graveyard, they were stopped again. A mighty crevice lay across their path, splintered and jagged. Some ancient movement of the earth bisected the chamber. Many of the tombs that lay along the crack were half toppled into the chasm, broken and splintered. Though the crevice spoke of a violent convulsion, it was diluted across a gulf of time. The lantern's light could just reach the far portion of the chamber across the divide.

Brek Gorunn inched forward and held his lamp over the edge.

"No bottom in sight," he said.

Ember joined Brek on the lip. She saw bits of crumbled stone and broken statuary fetched up on rough ledges farther down. One sarcophagus lay cracked completely open on a narrow ledge. It was empty, its former contents swallowed by the chasm.

The dwarf said, "The crevice looks to be about twenty or twenty five feet across. Too far to jump, at least for anyone but Ember."

Ember gathered her legs for the leap, eager to put it behind her. She felt a touch on her shoulder.

"Ember, hold on," Brek said. He pointed to the left. She could see a slender shaft of white stone jutting out over the chasm. "See that column? It bridges the chasm. Let's look at that before you risk jumping across."

"Don't think I can make it?" she asked.

"I am certain that you will make it," explained Brek Gorunn. "Then, there you'll be on the other side, vulnerable to any creature hiding over there in the gloom. You could be attacked while the rest of us are still stuck over here."

"Perhaps," conceded Ember.

Of course the dwarf was right. It wasn't like her to be impetuous, but the unrelieved darkness preyed on her mind.

The group moved to the fallen column. It bridged the crevice at an angle, and was visibly cracked. Brek ran his fingers across the stone, considering. He unlimbered his pack and rummaged through it, then produced the rope he'd purchased earlier in the city.

He said, "I don't trust this span. In case it gives out, a little insurance is best."

"Nebin, you're the lightest, you should cross first," Ember said.

When Brek didn't disagree, Nebin stepped up to the edge of the chasm. The dwarf tied the rope around the gnome's waist and secured the other end to a jutting piece of masonry.

"Make sure it's tight!" warned Nebin. "And leave plenty of slack, I don't want to be thrown off-balance by a snag on the rope."

The gnome peered across the chasm, then briskly stepped across the column, not looking down, his arms held out for balance. Ember smiled when he reached the far side. The gnome waved and undid the rope from around his waist.

Next went Hennet, then Ember carrying the lantern. She watched Brek Gorunn closely as he prepared to cross. He was the heaviest, and she worried. The dwarf undid the knot anchoring the rope to his side of the chasm. Once loose, he tied the free end around his waist and waved to her. She nodded, wrapped the rope twice around another marble obelisk on her side of the chasm, then tied the end to the same, heavy column. Holding the rope with both hands, she prepared to take up slack as the dwarf crossed by pulling the rope around the column.

Balance wasn't a problem. The dwarf's center of gravity was low enough that he could stroll across the bridge if he chose to. He decided instead that moving quickly would be best, as quickly as Ember could take in the rope. It took him only a few moments to reach the point where the crack was worst.

Ember saw Brek's eyes widen a heartbeat before the column snapped and he tumbled into darkness. The rope jerked in her hands like a living thing. She would have lost her grip completely if it hadn't been wound around the obelisk.

The sound of the broken stone thundering into the chasm mingled with incoherent yells from everyone. The anchored rope was taut and vibrating, and Ember could feel that it was swaying below the lip of the floor. She tied her end quickly around the tightened length of rope, then sped to the edge where Hennet knelt with the lantern. Brek swung on the end of the rope, twenty or so feet below them. The dwarf groaned.

As the ringing echoes of the crashing column finally abated, they were replaced by the sinister fluting, seductively light for all its dread melody. It emanated up from the night-haunted chasm. A miasma of fear rose with the sound and gripped Ember.

She heard the dwarf mutter a brief prayer. Then he said, straining his eyes below him, "I see . . . a blot of darkness. It's moving upward."

The fluting, too, was growing close. Ember realized then that it wasn't an instrument at all but the unearthly, terrible voice of whatever lurked below in the darkness. It was a sound long ago bereft of life and hope. Ember's mind became suddenly frantic.

It's coming for all of us, she realized. And Brek is hanging down there like bait!

The dwarf struggled to pull himself up. Ember saw a black, snakelike tendril slither up from the depths to touch Brek's boot.

"There's something down here!" bellowed the dwarf. "Pull me up, by Moradin's shaggy beard! Get me up!"

Ember, Hennet, and Nebin hauled madly on the rope. Fear lent a wild strength to their limbs, and with all three of them pulling, the dwarf shot up the side of the crevice. Seconds later, Brek's groping fingers reached the crumbling edge of the floor. Ember grabbed one hand and pulled the dwarf bodily over the lip.

Something followed after him.

A sinuous arm writhed its way up from the darkness. It was dead black and coated with oily mucous. It seemed a tentacle of living night, waking from some age-long communion with the subterranean void. Three more tendrils, identical to the first, flopped up to writhe across the floor like eyeless snakes seeking prey.

Behind the tendrils came the creature, dragging itself up and out of the crevice with inhuman strength. It was a blot of oily darkness where movement never ceased, a gargantuan mass of living, constantly slithering tentacles. Half hidden by the sliding tendrils, a sac of fluid sloshed at the core, emitting a crescendo of triumphant notes.

Brek Gorunn's massive hands pushed Ember back from the crevice. He was running, and she was running, too. They fled blindly away from the hideous piping sound. The awful music drove them in a mad dash without regard for their surroundings. The rope was left behind, along with anything else they had set down. None of that mattered. There was only death and terror behind them. By running they might hope to live.

Ember felt those things with dread certainty. She ran to save her own life. But as she caught up to Hennet and Nebin, she regained the presence of mind to match their slower pace.

Hennet still held the lantern. Shadows danced like imps across their path, making an ungainly pantomime with magnified arms and pumping legs. Sarcophagi and tombstones, crumbling with age, retreated on either side. Another hundred feet, and they plunged out of the vast mausoleum into a narrow tunnel.

The dread fluting ceased. Without its mental pressure, they checked their headlong flight. Ember felt as if a black fist released its hold on her stomach.

Nebin panted, "I hope we don't have to return this way."

Brek Gorunn, his skin uncharacteristically pale, responded, "Even if it proves the only possible escape, we'd do better to languish here. Moradin grant me strength, we woke something better left sleeping. If we leave it be, perhaps it will return to its evil slumber."

Hennet stated, "Forewarned is forearmed. We were startled, no more. Other than fear itself, it didn't do us any harm."

He gripped his Golden Wand. Ember wondered if the sorcerer wasn't drawing too much confidence from his Duel Arcane trophy.

"It didn't hurt us because we ran too fast, genius," said Nebin. "As my master often said, 'It's the tentacle you don't see that you should fear the most.' "

Hennet frowned.

"Regardless of the creature's true nature," broke in Ember, "we don't have to come back this way. We'll deal with Sosfane and her cult in the revived temple. After that we can leave through the temple's front door." Nor will we be coming back this way if we lose the fight, she concluded to herself.

"Did you hear that?" interrupted Brek Gorunn.

He looked back toward the tunnel mouth that opened into the subterranean mortuary. A second of silence was followed by a distant, fluting melody. Though faint, it sent a shiver up her spine.

Brek continued, "Perhaps we should move farther along this tunnel. No need to lure that cursed thing after us with chatter."

Ember nodded. She took the lantern back and handed it to the dwarf. Cautiously they advanced down the corridor.

Unlike the previous urn-lined corridors, this one was plain and carved directly from the surrounding stones without additional decoration. The drip of ages painted small mineral-rich stalagmites on the ceiling and long, colorful smears down the walls. The smell of damp and rot grew, and pools of water lay at their feet.

After many minutes of slow trudging through the unremarkable tunnel, Ember ventured, "What do you suppose all this was, before New Koratia was built, and before Nerull's priests claimed it?"

"Could have been the under-portions of a ruined surface city, I suppose," Brek offered. "The 'Ancient City' Nebin is so enraptured with."

"Or the upper-portions of a subterranean city?" questioned Hennet. "I've heard legends about evil elves who congregate far from the sun's reach."

Nebin, not to be outdone, said, "A treatise I read in my master's library hinted that these and other ruins represent some translocation of time—somewhere in the future, some terrible event destroys all life, and the ruins of civilization are buried in the deepest past."

"That's a thinker," replied Hennet.

Brek gave the gnome a bemused look.

Ember smiled and said, "That sounds a little far-fetched. What treatise was this, and what learned scholar was its author, Nebin?"

The gnome harrumphed and said nothing. Hennet and Ember shared a smile.

The advancing light of the lantern revealed a branch in the tunnel ahead, a **Y** leading to left and right.

"Which way?" inquired Ember.

The dwarf stood quiet, looking and sniffing into each dark opening, neither of which seemed particularly different from the other in Ember's estimation. The dwarf puzzled, pulling thoughtfully on his beard, and looked for some sign or telltale rune.

Finally, Brek Gorunn said, "We should go right. If we have to retrace our route, it pays to be consistent—we should go right at every branch. Plus, I don't like the smell to the left. It somehow puts me in mind of that flute player."

That was enough for Ember. They took the right-hand passage. By this time, the damp was so extreme that a thin layer of pooled, stagnant water formed a continuous slurry on the muddy floor. Ember promised to buy herself boots to keep in her pack for just such occasions—her order preferred open-toed sandals. Sandals are not suited for catacomb trekking, she thought.

"I hope the water doesn't keep rising," commented Nebin.

Ember realized that because of his stature, he would be affected more than the others. Still, she'd rather be short than feel the muddy sludge squeezing between her toes with every step.

Suddenly the lantern's light fell on a closed stone door blocking their passage ahead. Ember moved up, motioning the others to silence. She placed one ear to the door, listening, and heard nothing but her own heartbeat.

Pulling away, she told the others, "Be ready," and she opened the door.

A noise as of stone on stone echoed down the hall.

"Oh, shards!" she gasped as the entire length of the passage where they stood swung down beneath them.

For the second time that day, Brek Gorunn felt himself falling. What had been a slick, muddy, but level corridor was transformed into a slick, muddy chute. He and his companions helplessly slid, one after another, and dropped onto a slimy, muddy floor. Brek didn't know how far he'd fallen, but it was a hard landing even with the mud as a cushion. It hadn't been so bad for Hennet, Brek guessed, because the human had the advantage of landing on the dwarf.

Lying on his back while the others groaned and struggled to regain their footing on the treacherous floor, Brek surveyed his surroundings. They were in a pit, about twenty feet on a side. The ceiling was just visible in the lantern's light, placing it about thirty feet up, Brek estimated. The chute above snapped back up into its former position high above the floor, trapping them all in a tight box of stone. He scanned the walls; no exit was visible on any surface. He checked himself for injuries, found none, then rose to help the others who weren't as durable as dwarves.

"Oh, perfect!" grumbled Nebin, as Brek helped him up from a facedown position in the mud.

His elaborate coat was sopped and soiled. The others were back on their feet already. The lantern revealed bones of small creatures, cave vermin most likely, mixed in with the mud and water puddles filling the bottom of their prison. Besides the bones of vermin, a lone humanoid skull sat half submerged in the shallow muck. Its presence spoke volumes about the position they had tumbled into.

"We're lucky this shaft is not half-filled with water," the dwarf noted. "There must be drainage of some sort."

Brek nudged the skull with his boot.

"Drainage?" said Nebin. "Who cares? What a useless thing to say . . . hello!"

The gnome's rant was derailed, apparently when he noticed large runes on one wall. Brek Gorunn frowned, beginning to feel downright testy. He decided that Nebin was lucky he'd stopped speaking when he did; this was no time to test anyone's temper. He gave the skull another kick, splashing it across the chamber. He hoped they wouldn't all end up the same as the skull: lost, trapped, starved, and finally dead.

"What do the runes say, Nebin?" asked Ember.

"I can't make them out. But I will." The gnome gestured, releasing a pinch of salt into the air from his pouch, and incanted a few arcane syllables. His eyes gleamed with ethereal luminance, and he read: " 'You have chosen the Testing Pit of Lo-Riao. Your arrival here indicates your agreement to be tested. Choose your measure: Test by Strife, or Test by Wit.' "

The gnome scratched his head and said, "Lo-Riao? Must have something to do with the ancient city."

The others shook their heads, indicating that they were equally unfamiliar with the name.

The gnome continued, "There is a miniature hand print under the word 'Strife' and the same under the word 'Wit'."

The dwarf, beginning to feel herded in a direction he did not care for, said, "Choice? What are you going on about? I choose to get out of this pit, not engage in some ancient guessing game!"

Hennet noted, "It is unfortunate we left the rope in the crevice of the flute player."

His timing was bad. The dwarf shot Hennet a lethal look while he formulated a heated retort.

Ember stepped between them and said, "I'd like the rope, and a dry suit of clothes, and some decent boots, but we have none of those things. The only way we will get out of here is by working together, and by 'here' I don't mean just this pit. Now is not the time to fall on one another with bared teeth."

"Tell that to the sorcerer," mumbled Brek Gorunn.

"That's enough, Brek," Ember shot back. "We need your help and your strength, here more than anywhere."

She was right, Brek knew. Underground, the others were in an alien environment, but it felt like home to him. Not his home, exactly, with slime and fluting monstrosities, but it was a delving just the same.

"I'm fine, Ember," Brek replied. "It's just that he did fall on me, when we tumbled down that chute."

Nebin giggled. "You mean Hennet landed on you? I wish I had," he added, rubbing his shoulder.

"I guess I did," Hennet admitted. "Sorry about that. It was unintentional. I grabbed for anything to hang onto as we slid down the chute and got hold of you."

He looked intently at his feet smothered in the mud. Brek Gorunn coughed, feeling warm under his armor. Apologies, coming from anyone, made him uncomfortable.

"Forget it."

"That's better," said Ember. "Now, I am going to try climbing out of the shaft. I'd rather not activate some ancient test about which we know nothing, and trust it to provide our exit."

Nebin looked defiant but offered no counterargument.

Ember approached the wall, and Brek sorted through his pack, hoping to find a useful piece of equipment.

"Too bad I don't have a lifting spell," lamented Nebin. "Once, I had a scroll that granted spiderlike climbing ability, but no more."

Ember nodded, then shot a glance at Hennet. The sorcerer just shook his head.

Brek watched Ember trying to find a finger- or toe-hold on the slick wall, but she had little success. The masonry was too well fitted, despite its age. He had been afraid of that—the chamber was well made with strength and solidity. She tried a few running leaps, attempting to reach a higher point along the wall.

After a few fruitless attempts, she paused, breathing hard, and said, "All right, if we're forced to activate a test, which one?"

Brek said, "The test by strife," just as Nebin said, "Test by wit, of course."

Brek paused and glared at the gnome, who had a similar look on his face.

"I feel we could pass either test," said Ember. "Hennet, your vote decides the issue. What will it be?"

Hennet mused, "Strife would be the most straightforward."

Brek smiled, and he reached for the shaft of his warhammer. The sorcerer had a keen head on his shoulders.

"But," continued Hennet, "we can expect strife and then some when we finally break into the temple. Perhaps we should preserve our strength for that encounter. For that reason, I choose 'wit'."

Brek Gorunn reevaluated his opinion of the sorcerer's instincts, but stayed silent.

"Fine," said Ember. "Be ready, everyone. Nebin, please activate the test. Let's hope it still works."

"And let's hope it is not part of some more elaborate trap," worried Brek.

Nebin studied the small hand prints, shrugged, and touched one of them, presumably the one below the rune for 'wit,' though of course Brek couldn't read it.

The skull, the very one Brek Gorunn earlier kicked, spoke. It lay on its side, fetched up in a corner of the shaft. Its voice was harsh, grating, if a bit muffled from its new position.

"Answer me; be free," spoke the skull. "Fail; remain with me.

"A novitiate of dread Lo-Riao seeks to enter the Door of Midnight ahead of his time and without knowledge of the secret password. The novitiate observes a master of Lo-Riao pass the door freely. When he knocked, a dread voice behind the Door of Midnight thundered, 'Twelve.' The master answered, 'Six,' and was allowed to pass. When another master approached and knocked, the voice screamed, 'Six.' The second master answered, 'Three,' and was allowed to pass. The novitiate, emboldened by the pattern he thought he saw, approached the Door of Midnight and knocked. The voice behind the door intoned, 'Ten!' The novitiate answered, 'Five.' For his failure, the novitiate's essence was absorbed by the flautist who guards the Door of Midnight.

"How should the novitiate have answered?" concluded the skull.

After it finished speaking, it lay inert in the corner, empty sockets staring blindly ahead.

Nebin coughed and said, "I hope all this business about Lo-Riao and the Door of Midnight is secondary to the real answer, otherwise we're in trouble, my friends. I've never heard of either."

Hennet said, "It is some sort of mathematical trick."

The sorcerer furrowed his brow as he looked at the inert skull.

Brek Gorunn mentally ran through the skull's speech. He'd have made the same choice as the novitiate—it seemed clear that the first two masters had simply responded with a countersign equal to half of the number given out by the door. But, when the novitiate did responded with half of ten, the pattern was broken.

He said aloud, "The pattern isn't half the first number, that's clear."

Hennet nodded. "Yes, too simple. All this talk of midnight and dread voices makes me wonder whether magic isn't involved?"

Nebin said, "Maybe Lo-Riao is a god of the ancient city. What if the formula is part of a ritual lost to time? We won't hit upon it by chance."

"This is a test of wit, not memory," said Ember. "If that's true, we should not look to old rituals and secret numbers, arbitrarily applied, for our answer. There must be a pattern we can puzzle out."

Brek silently agreed. They sat silent for a while, each trying to work the puzzle according to their own predispositions. Brek wondered if it was simpler than he was trying to make it.

How many letters are there in six? he wondered. Three, of course . . .

"Wait, I see another pattern!" he burst out. "It is mathematical, as Hennet said first, but it's even simpler than we first supposed. See? How many letters are in the word twelve? Six! And in the word six there are three letters. Those were the countersigns given by the masters."

"So, if the Door of Midnight gives the sign 'ten'," said Hennet, "the counter-sign must be three; there are three letters in the word ten."

Ember grinned at the dwarf.

"Is your answer 'three'?" broke in the skull, suddenly attentive.

Ember looked around, then said, "Three is our answer."

The skull said nothing, and the silence stretched.

The floor below them lurched, then began rising. A haze of dust, loosened from the walls and ceiling, filled the air. The pools of liquid on the floor drained away. The floor lifted thirty feet or more than stopped, just as they all began to worry about the approaching ceiling. At that height, they could see an exit that was hidden from below. It was situated on the side of the shaft opposite from where they had entered.

"Brek Gorunn, old dog, who would have guessed you're a first rate riddle master?" exclaimed Nebin. "We're out!"

The methodical exploration of the ancient labyrinth
agreed with Hennet. He relished it, unlike his friend Nebin. The
gnome declared on more than one occasion his wish to be free
of the dark ways. The slow revelation of hidden paths forgotten
below the earth, leading to further mysterious chambers, tunnels,
tombs, and deeper passages, thrilled his sense of adventure.
Danger threatened every step, but of course that was the spice.
What was the lost purpose of these ancient halls? Were the
delvers humanoid, or did they belong to some older, pre-
humanoid species? It was fun to speculate.

They bypassed a chamber whose ceiling was upheld by stat-
ues carved to resemble giant men bearing a great burden. They
walked along a hall where corroded metal plates in the ceiling
buzzed and gleamed as they passed, but which offered no other
clue as to their purpose. They walked through a tiny waterfall that
issued from a shaft far above, and drained away through a side passage that led steeply down, possibly to join some sunless sea of
myth. Or so Hennet liked to imagine.

Even now they walked a passage hung with the tatters of time-lost tapestries, Brek in front holding the gleaming lantern aloft. A garble of whispered voices issued from the very stone beneath their feet. When they first heard the noises, the company stopped and thoroughly investigated, but could find no inherent threat. Thus, they walked on, despite the susurrus of voices speaking in tongues long dead on the surface.

For a long stretch—since the Test of Wit in fact—nothing assailed their passage. Such was the sorcerer's thought when they came to a side door along the passage. Bones of some past traveler lay strewn before the door. Here he had apparently met his end. The catacombs were moist and given to rot, and the traveler's possessions were decomposed, but a dagger still glinted, untouched by time. The nearby door was rent and notched, as if the traveler had spent his last hours desperately trying to force his way through. If so, he had failed in that attempt and died far from light and hope.

Nebin ventured, "Why do you suppose he wanted to pass this door? Is our way the same, to reach the revived temple?"

Brek Gorunn looked at the door, then forward down the hall they had been traversing, and said, "My gut tells me this door is not our path. But it conceals something, or so this poor fellow believed."

"We should open the door ourselves, to see what we can see," broke in Hennet. This was exactly the sort of thing he loved. "Perhaps a treasury, or a library filled with the lore of times forgotten?"

He threw in the library in an attempt to get Nebin interested.

"Or a demon bound with spells of somnolence, until disturbed," said Brek Gorunn. "It may be both, or neither, but it is not our quest. Later, we may return when other needs are met. It would be foolhardy to turn aside now, wasting our strength when we will soon have such need of it."

"Brek Gorunn is right, Hennet," said Ember. She put a hand on his shoulder as if commiserating. Her touch was enough to convince him.

Besides, he realized the wisdom of Brek's words. "At least let's gather this poor fellows belongings," he said. "We might learn something of his purpose."

So saying, he retrieved the dagger. He turned it over in his hands, and the others drew close. Beautiful, he thought. The handle was carved to resemble a unicorn, and the blade, its horn. Its ageless appearance suggested preservation only magic could explain. Testing that hypothesis was easy enough—Hennet concentrated on the dagger and felt the answering pulse of enchantment. It wasn't an overpowering response, but it was definite.

The sorcerer looked up to his companions and said, "This dagger is magical."

A harsh voice from farther up the hallway said, "Then hand it over!"

Hennet started, nearly dropping the dagger, as the others whirled around. Farther up along the passage, a band of men appeared, unshuttering their lamps and drawing their swords.

There were perhaps half a dozen of them. The four in the front, three humans and a halfling, waved swords as they came on, two by two down the corridor. Two elves in the rear held cocked bows.

Another man, better dressed than the others and standing behind the elves, called out, "The dagger, and your other valuables. We're the Raiding Lions. I'm Jeelsen. If you've heard of us, you know that we are merciful to those who surrender up their wealth to us when asked."

Brek Gorunn cursed, "By Moradin's overflowing tankard, what are you doing down here?"

Nebin called out, "Actually, we haven't heard of you, Jellyfish!"

Hennet elbowed the gnome in the ribs, hard.

"The name," screamed the brigand, "is *Jeelsen!* If you haven't heard of us, then know now that while we are merciful to some, to those who give us trouble we are bloodthirsty to the last. Which shall we visit on you? Mercy, or death? Either way, we'll have your valuables. Surrender now and live!"

Brek muttered, "There must be other entrances to the catacombs besides the one we used."

Hennet could only agree. At least, none of those menacing them in the narrow hall carried overt Nerullan symbology.

Nebin whispered, "Who does this poser think he's fooling? Hennet, ensorcel him, I'll take out the rest."

Ember raised an eyebrow. Hennet knew why; it wasn't like the gnome to be so brash. Hennet studied his friend, and saw the way he possessively clutched his spellbook.

Brek Gorunn said, "Those archers can do much damage from a distance, while the swordsmen hold us off. Perhaps we should pay their toll."

Ember looked at the dwarf, then at Hennet and Nebin, and said, "I'm not about to give them Loku's Bracers, the relics of my vanquished chapter. Without our equipment, we would have to turn back from our quest, and there's no way out behind us. I'm with Nebin. We must fight."

Hennet, never one to back down from a challenge, nodded grimly.

Jeelsen, seeing their impromptu conference, apparently misread their hesitation.

He yelled, "Yes, yes, you know I speak the truth. Save yourselves some trouble. Am I answered?"

Nebin shouted, "You are!"

The gnome flicked a scroll from his belt and began incanting. Brek unlimbered a crossbow and scrambled to fit a bolt and pull back the crank.

He yelled, "Watch those archers! I'll peg the swordsmen."

Hennet's blood beat in his ears. Brek and Ember took the front rank in the narrow corridor, while he and Nebin stood behind.

Hennet yelled, "You picked your victims badly this time!"

Actually he had no illusions about his own power and his inexperience in the world, but perhaps his bold speech, backed up by aggressive action, would give the bandits pause. He called up his own power. Magic was in his blood, and he loved wielding it. Giving it a shape and a name, he let go a glittering, ruby ray toward Jeelsen.

Ember leaped forward, directly toward the swordsmen. Hennet tensed, then gasped in surprise as she deftly tumble-rolled past them, avoiding their sudden, wild swings. Arrows from the bow-armed elves whined past her spinning form to snap against the wall and floor. Then she was past them, too. Before Hennet quite knew how, she stood next to Jeelsen. The bandit leader recoiled in surprise.

That was when Hennet's magical bolts struck the bandit leader, sending him gasping and reeling backward. Ember followed up, unleashing a spinning kick that knocked Jeelsen flat. Twin streamers of smoke rose from his clothing where Hennet's spell had hit him.

Nebin finished his incantation, and the two swordsmen at the front collapsed to the floor, asleep. The four left on their feet wavered.

Brek Gorunn, who had finally finished cocking his crossbow, pointed at the leading swordsman and said, "Run."

The archers and swordsmen, seeing Jeelsen prostrate and smoking, ran back down the corridor the way they came. Jeelsen, despite his pain, called after them to no effect. Ember nudged him with her foot, as if to remind the bandit leader of her presence.

Jeelsen suddenly changed tactics, exclaiming, "Mercy! We

made a grave error. Oh, yes, most grave. We didn't know . . . we didn't realize you were so powerful . . . please, mercy!"

Ember nudged the man with her foot again. Hennet saw that by the way she clenched her jaw, she was restraining herself from delivering a stronger blow.

"Get up," she said. "Wake your men, and leave. If we meet you or any of your men again in these catacombs, or hear of you attacking anyone else, you'll have us to reckon with and we won't be merciful. Do you understand me?"

Jeelsen rose unsteadily to his feet and said, "I understand."

Still holding his cocked crossbow, Brek Gorunn added, "Fear makes you agreeable now. When we've gone, remember that we showed you mercy when you deserved none. Seek a new path, or your reward will be ashes in your mouth. Even Moradin may be merciful to the repentant."

Hennet wondered at the dwarf's sudden sermonizing. It was a tack he hadn't used before. Then again, he'd never fought human foes with the dwarf before.

Jeelsen, not quite sure what to make of the dwarf's speech, murmured, "You are so right. Of course, I'll repent."

Without a glance at his men who lay sleeping from Nebin's spell, he turned and trotted down the stone corridor after the others, grabbing his lamp as he passed. The bobbing light dwindled into the distance.

"I don't know why I waste Moradin's teaching on one such as him," Brek Gorunn said. "Incompetence is its own reward—that's another of the Dwarffather's teachings, my friends."

The dwarf laughed, uncocking his crossbow.

Ember rejoined them before the door, stepping carefully over the sleeping forms, and said, "A swift fight—a good omen, I think. Let's continue. These louts can take their chances here after sleeping off their poor decision."

"Should we interrogate one of the sleepers," asked Hennet, "to see if they know anything about the temple?"

Ember paused, her brow creased. She shook her head. "No, I'd rather they continue to think we're tomb raiders like themselves. We can't kill them in cold blood, and I'd hate to let them know our purpose in case they get ahead of us and give warning."

He nodded. She was right. He didn't kid himself—at this point, he'd find it hard to disagree with her, no matter what she said.

"We just scared off a roving band of brigands without taking a bruise!" exulted Nebin.

Hennet grinned and said, "We do make a good team, don't you think, Ember?" He glanced at Ember, smiling. She winked back. Then they readjusted their gear and moved on.

Ember felt they were close. Brek Gorunn confirmed it. His dwarven instincts concerning stone and the earth seemed supernatural, they were so finely tuned. Even some of her own abilities, and certainly those of her teachers, verged on and sometimes crossed the line from ordinary to extraordinary, Ember reflected.

But the passage Brek led them down was blocked by water. She watched Brek, wondering which way he'd point them next. The dwarf was baffled.

"The map indicates clearly that this is the fastest way," he said. "If we have to backtrack, we'll lose hours!"

The stone walls of the tunnel opened up on either side into what seemed a natural cavern that was far larger than the lamp's small circle of illumination. The floor descended to the edge of a subterranean lake. Its water was so perfectly still and so inky black that it looked almost like a gigantic mirror laid on the floor. The sound of splashing, however, indicated that somewhere in

the distance, the water was moving. Of more immediate concern
was a glimmer of green light twinkling out on the lake. In the
gloom, it was impossible to judge the distance from the shore to
the unidentified light.

Ember edged down to the pool. Something caught her eye on
the left side of the cavern.

"Brek, please bring the lamp down here."

The dwarf obliged. With the light, Ember spied a slender stone
ledge running around the side of the cavern. It was close to the
water and difficult to see. At the near end the ledge was only
about two feet across, and the edges were partly crumbled.
Whether it continued on that way for its whole length was
anyone's guess. It was the only way forward. The dwarf had not
steered them wrong, and Ember clapped him on the back.

"This way," she said. "I'll go first, then Brek with the light.
Hennet and Nebin bring up the rear—Nebin, watch behind. We
don't want to be surprised out on this catwalk."

The gnome gulped, nodding.

Silently, clutching at the rocky wall to the left, they went in
single file along the ledge. Indeed, there were many places where
the path was crumbled nearly to nothing. Luckily, the gaps were
small enough that a single step was sufficient to get past, even for
the gnome. Ember wasn't worried about herself here. It was Brek
Gorunn, with his broad shoulders and heavy armor, that caused
her concern.

Splashes echoed again across the lake. A quick check behind
confirmed that all her friends were accounted for.

From the rear, Nebin whispered, "Now don't tell me you all
didn't hear that?"

Ember cocked her head and heard another series of splashes.
A sad melody sounding like a flute wafted out from the cold darkness behind them.

"Oh, shards!" yelled Nebin. "It's been following us. Go, go, go!"

So saying, the gnome tried to worm his way around Hennet and nearly knocked both of them into the still water.

"Nebin, if you push me in so help me . . . ," began Hennet.

"Quickly!" hissed Ember from the lead.

Following her own command, she turned and redoubled her earlier pace, praying the dwarf suffered no misstep. If he fell, he'd be lost. Now was not the time to mount a water rescue. She didn't want to meet that hideous, tentacled thing again, and especially not while trapped on a ledge.

They all followed her, and so, too, did the fluting. Ripples, as of something moving out on the lake, began washing against the foot of the ledge. The fear she remembered so clearly from the nightmare at the crevice clawed anew at the edges of her mind.

The path opened into a larger space, and Ember rushed forward from the ledge, gasping, looking for any avenue of escape. The others were close on her heels and had the same thoughts in mind. But the space seemed only a cubbyhole, a room-sized niche in the side of the cavern.

Somehow they all spied the alcove at the back of the landing at the same time and rushed forward. To their horror, it was not a pathway but only a small, dead-end hollow space. The only way out was to continue around the lake on the ledge, and that meant more of the horrid fluting.

Besides the horror of the tentacled thing, Ember had been keeping one eye on the green light. They were noticeably closer to it now. In fact, it was close enough that she could see its glow reflected off the damp stone walls of the cavern.

Suddenly the light dimmed to nothing. Ember realized that something must have blocked the entrance to the niche, trapping them inside.

Tentacles wavered toward them in the small chamber, twitching in time to that hideous, unnatural fluting. The sound was utterly devoid of life, like the voice of death calling in the night. It seemed to come from a void, and it beckoned them to its realm beyond terror.

Ember believed her last, desperate hour had arrived. She moved forward, uncertain what she could do against such a creature, but preferring death to torment. Beside her, Brek Gorunn held forth his warhammer, praying aloud to Moradin for the strength to prevail against such unholy might. Nebin pointed his trusty wand at the blot of evil, his face set and grim. Hennet drew the Golden Wand, his eyes steely.

Ember inched forward.

Interlaced with the ghastly music, she suddenly heard a voice.

It was an inhuman sound created by the lilting tones, and it said, "Give back what you have stolen." Ember hesitated, confused.

Nebin squeaked out, "We haven't stolen anything! Leave us be!"

The mass filled all the opening and bulged inward. The music swelled, and with it the voice.

It said again, "Give back. Give back what you have stolen. The Door of Midnight swings wide, unless the thief returns the key."

Her voice shaking, Ember asked, "What did the thief take?"

A dozen tentacles wormed across the cramped space as the voice said, "The horn blade."

"The unicorn dagger!" cried Hennet as he yanked the gleaming blade from his belt. He flipped it through the air toward the monstrosity. "Take it!"

Darkness converged on the dagger, hiding it from view. The moment the weapon disappeared, the music died.

A final note whispered, "You may go," then silence returned.

The darkness receded from the lantern's glow like a physical creature. Perhaps it was. When it was gone, so was the dagger.

Ember breathed heavily. Perhaps her last battle wasn't upon her after all.

She smiled tentatively and said, "Was that a good omen?"

Everyone laughed, the tension broken. Nebin cast himself on the floor in relief.

"Perhaps we were wrong about that fellow we found lying near the door," said Hennet. "I guess that dagger wasn't his, though we found it near his remains. He must have taken it from some tomb or reliquary. Perhaps from beyond that door—could it be the Door of Midnight? If it wasn't his, it wasn't mine to take, either. I hope we returned it to its rightful owner."

Ember placed a hand on both of Hennet's shoulders, facing him. "I'd say you saved us."

Hennet took one of her hands in both of his and held it. His touch was firm, dry, and she treasured it.

"Not to interrupt this moment," said the dwarf, "but we're close to the center." Brek Gorunn stood at the edge of the niche where the creature had so recently been. He looked out across the water and the faint, green trail glimmering like a path to the nearby glow. "The green glow just ahead could well mark the porch of the revived temple."

"Whether it does or doesn't, I need to rest," said Nebin. "I've had as much as I can take in one day. If we're so close, let's rest a while, then go on at full strength afterward."

Brek nodded. "I can barely think, for memory of that fluting sound. That music will haunt me for years."

He looked at Ember, who mentally recounted the hours that had passed since they entered the catacombs. Everyone had sustained bruises and cuts in the fall down the chute. The mages had nearly exhausted their spells along the way and needed time to

rest if only to refocus their energy. Ember was tired simply from
so many hours of walking through darkness at high alert. Their
narrow escape from the tentacled monstrosity had earned them
a rest.

"Set camp," she said.

Their narrow sanctuary was bare of any adornment, debris, or
other clues to its original purpose. For now, it served as the perfect shelter. Bedrolls and provisions were retrieved them from
packs. Ember's mat had seen better days, but she still found it
comfortable; she'd slept on much worse. Brek set the lantern in
the corner, refilled the oil, and turned the wick low. Ember realized that she had come to regard the lantern and its welcome light
almost as another member of their group.

Brek Gorunn volunteered for the first watch. He sat on the
floor, near the alcove opening, humming dwarven chants under
his breath. Ember tried to sleep, lulled by the dwarf's murmuring, the glimmering shadows thrown by the lamp, Nebin's snores,
and Hennet's deep, easy breathing.

Hennet started suddenly awake—had someone tapped him?
It was Ember, waking him for his turn on watch. The dwarf and
the gnome were bundled in their bedrolls along one wall, turned
away from the light of the lantern. Ember sat near him. The sorcerer sat up and yawned.

"All quiet?" asked Hennet sleepily.

"All quiet," confirmed Ember.

She watched him, her eyes hidden in shadow, but with a small
smile touching her lips.

"Great. I'm good. I'll wake Nebin in a few hours. Get some
sleep."

Ember nodded, but said, "I'm not sleepy. I've been meditating as I sat here, so I'm rested. I'll keep you company during your watch, if you like."

"I'd like nothing better!"

"Good. Perhaps you and I can talk a little."

"About what?"

Ember mused, then said, "I thought perhaps you could tell me more of your past journeys. I'm still curious about Nebin and the 'red lever' you referred to last night in the Cuttlestone."

Hennet laughed quietly, absurdly pleased she remembered his words. It seemed as if he had spoken them weeks ago. He pulled a wine skin from his pack and shared some with Ember. The stone where they sat was cold, and the wine helped warm their backsides, or at least it seemed so.

Hennet began, his voice a bit hoarse at first, "Well, it's a silly story after all. An alchemist known to both Nebin and I asked us to visit him in his home. He wanted our help on a certain matter of enchantment. The details are unimportant. The moment he left us alone in his laboratory, Nebin began riffling through things. That's when he found the lever. I knew right away what he was thinking, and warned him off. Of course he wouldn't listen. The next thing we knew, we were being chiseled out of an alchemical preservative. Two weeks had passed in the blink of an eye as we stood frozen in place. Nebin dumped a full load of the stuff on top of us. We're lucky neither of us suffocated."

Ember laughed quietly. Hennet wondered at her sudden closeness. He stopped himself from jumping to conclusions. Just because they were finally alone, and Ember chose that moment to make small talk—well, what of it? Likely she just wanted to talk, as she had indicated. But where his head insisted on reading nothing into the lamp-side chat, his heart had an entirely different interpretation.

When Ember drew close, kissing him on the lips, he knew his heart was right all along.

The lantern's light revealed her face a lighter shade against the dark stone walls behind her, but not so dark as her hair. Her eyes were as bright as stars.

"We have a little time," she whispered.

14

Nebin felt enlivened after the rest, ready for anything.

He snapped his fingers, laughing, "I'm even ready for another flute-playing phantom."

He chuckled, waiting for Hennet's censuring look, disapproving of his over-exuberance. But Hennet and Ember were paying attention only to each other, not to him. He decided he could grandstand later, when his audience was ready to appreciate his wit.

When camp was struck, they again moved out on the narrow ledge. The vast cavern remained dark but for the emerald beacon. The black water was perfectly calm. They continued their interrupted journey on the ledge that seemed to circled the water. Nebin felt much better when they finally reached the green radiance.

The light gleamed from the mouth of a tunnel that opened on the lake. The gnome estimated the tunnel was roughly opposite from where they'd entered the cavern. Water from the lake encroached the corridor, but it was shallow enough for them to splash through.

The pale glow seeped from the very stone like condensation, beading the walls with motes of sick radiance. Black water lapped on the floor of the corridor, still and fetid. He could hardly bear the stagnant stink of it as they trooped forward. Thankfully, about thirty paces in they arrived at the tunnel's terminus. An iron door blocked the passage. Disturbing scenes were welded onto the door's face, which Nebin avoided looking at too closely. The skull and scythe symbol of Nerull was welded into the very center of the door in raised relief. A dark gemstone gleamed dully in one eye socket, but the other was hollow. No keyhole or pull ring was visible on the door. Nebin realized that this was probably the back entrance to the revived temple of Nerull, the Reaper of Flesh.

"No one has come this way in a long, long time," said Brek Gorunn. "I doubt this water has stirred in years. I think we've achieved the surprise we sought."

Nebin sloshed forward, sending small waves to ripple through the pool. He was glad to find the water shallower near the door. He pushed up his goggles and squinted at the relief-carved skull.

"Is the skull important?" wondered Ember.

Nebin wondered the same thing. "What kind of gem is that, do you think?"

He reached out, tapping it. Nothing happened.

Brek Gorunn said, "Nebin! Be careful, will you?"

Nebin nodded, half listening. "Sure . . . Say, maybe this is some sort of key."

He touched the empty socket, and the dwarf's intake of breath was audible. Again, nothing happened.

The gnome scratched his chin.

"Maybe pull the other one out?" ventured Hennet.

Brek Gorunn glared at Nebin, stroked the head of his war-hammer, and said, "Or, if we're just going to poke and prod our way into every trap and alarm along the path anyway, I could save some time and just hammer the door off its hinges."

Ember shook her head and said, "Before we start getting on one another's nerves again, lets try a few simple ideas. For instance, why is one eye socket hollow, but the other filled?

"Try this," she continued. "Put something in the hollow socket. A small gem, like the other, perhaps." So saying, she reached into an inner pocket in her vest and drew out a small gemstone. "Agate. Not too valuable, but maybe worth a shot."

The monk tossed the stone to the gnome. Nebin caught the agate, examined it briefly, then pressed it into the hollow socket.

Nothing.

Brek Gorunn grumbled, "Is the beard-tangled door even locked?"

"That's a good question," admitted Nebin.

He pushed on the door.

A faint, emerald glitter woke in the skull's stone eye. They heard a click, and the door began swinging silently open. Ember and Brek both looked at Nebin in surprise. He realized he may have been premature. Slightly embarrassed, he snatched the agate back from the skull and slipped it into his coat pocket as the door opened wide.

"Be ready!" whispered Ember.

She fell into *bahng ah jah se*, the right guarding stance, and watched the opening widen. The time for subtlety was reaching an end. Nebin scuttled back from the door, pulling his goggles down over his eyes.

"Is everyone ready?" she whispered.

She looked to Hennet first. The sorcerer flicked his wrist, and the Golden Wand fell easily into it, promising potent electrical displays. Brek produced the oil he'd purchased at the Wizard's Hoard and poured it over the head of his warhammer. The weapon absorbed all the oil instantly, then glimmered with a dull, inner light.

Bright light spilled from the room beyond. Ember blinked as her eyes adjusted to the powerful illumination.

The chamber beyond the door was expansive. The ceiling rose smoothly into a dome high above the floor. Virulent emerald light pulsed through the mortared stone walls and played lewdly over the signs and figures carved on them. Lambent rivulets of radiance gathered and flowed down the walls, creating a shallow pool of brightness in the center of the floor. Within the pool of light, things moved—familiar, sluglike things. They lay in the light as if bathing, and perhaps they were. Their high, piping voices cried rhythmically to the cadence of the pulsing illumination. They were ghostly, however, insubstantial, as if they were not entirely real, or not entirely . . . there.

People stood silhouetted against the glowing pool, partly occluding the writhing forms. Two of the figures were covered in funerary wrappings—they were undead. Only one figure was female—a silvery-haired woman wearing a hooded, skull-encrusted cloak. Perhaps it was Sosfane, the mastermind behind all their recent woe. Several men stood nearby, dressed in loose robes and wearing red half-masks. Cultists, she realized, and probably all trained in the way of hand, foot, and fist.

One of the men wore no mask, and his face seemed familiar. The memory flooded back to Ember—it was Aganon, the man Hennet defeated in the final round of the Duel Arcane! She looked back and saw similar recognition come to Hennet and Nebin.

Brek Gorunn's plan to come upon the temple from the rear worked better than she could have imagined. Unless she missed her guess, they'd stumbled into the heart of the revived temple. Better yet, their arrival hadn't yet been noticed. She decided to wait. The worshipers would likely disperse after the ritual's conclusion, and it would be better to attack them separately, rather than all at once.

The woman in the hooded cloak spoke, raising her voice as she chanted, "By your beneficence Great Lord of the Night, Reaper of all Flesh, Foe of Light, Hater of Life, and King of Death Renewed, accept this sacrifice. Send us your voice to walk among us again, so that we might know your will fully and act with your grim blessing."

The mummies groaned their agreement, while Aganon and the red-masked monks repeated, "With your grim blessing."

The piping of the creatures caught in the light intensified. One of the half-slugs began shaking. Its ululations reached an ear-splitting pitch. As if flicked by an unseen giant's finger, it tumbled out of the pool of light, leaving a slick trail of slime along the stone floor. Unlike the shadowy forms left behind, this one was now all too real. The death god had sent its gift in the form of an abyssal child. And unless Ember's eyes were deceived, the abyssal child was larger than the one they had barely beaten on the road to New Koratia.

The creature sniffed with its horrible infantlike head, then swiveled its body. Its eyes locked onto Ember's and she knew their secret was discovered.

The creature screeched in a demented little girl's voice, "Nerull commands the death of those who look upon these proceedings. They defile this unholy temple, who have refused his oath, who have not received the sacrament of Nerull."

The time of waiting and watching was past. It was time for battle.

The silver-haired woman called loudly, "Intruders in the shrine! To me, my loyal monks!"

With a flick of her hand, she discarded her cloak. Beneath it, she wore a belted half-robe, loose pants, and sandals. Terrible figures were tattooed into her skin. Her eyes shone with vicious intent, fixing on Ember.

"Sosfane?" asked Ember.

The woman slowly smiled in acknowledgement.

"Ah, another monk from my old Order, come to take the Oath? Too late! You should have joined earlier. Now I can offer you only death."

"We rooted out your influence in the Enabled Hand with Vobod's defeat," replied Ember. "We're here to finish the job at the source. Your minutes are numbered, evil one."

Sosfane scoffed. "Your meddling has cost us time, nothing more. Soon enough, the Enabled Hand will return to the fold. This time, they will do Nerull's bidding forevermore." She motioned to the red-masked monks and cloth-wrapped mummies around her. "Kill her, my cenobites. Kill them all."

The undead grunted and lumbered forward, their hands extended and grasping. The red-masked monks grinned and fanned out as they advanced.

Brek Gorunn dashed past Ember into the chamber. He should have charged seconds earlier, before the summoning was complete, but it was too late for should-have-dones. Once in, he stopped short, holding his warhammer over his head.

He called out, "Give way, husks of the once-living! Turn your faces and be destroyed!"

His hammer blazed with golden light, temporarily washing

out the greenish glow all around him. One of the creatures barely noticed the holy command and moved in to batter the advancing dwarf with fingers stiffened into a permanent claw. The other mummy, however, puffed into a thousand motes of dust, instantly obliterated by Moradin's holy influence. The dwarf yelled triumphantly, even as the remaining mummy swiped at him with a withered hand.

Brek fell back—he knew that the touch of these animated monsters carried a foul, rotting disease. He saw the corpse's face, partly hidden beneath centuries-old funeral wrappings, open its mouth and exhale a puff of rotten air into his face. He stumbled back another step, but as he did so he raised his warhammer with both hands.

"Be dead, damn you!" screamed the dwarf.

His hammer crashed down on the creature's head. The mummy's empty, dried skull shattered to pieces, leaving only tattered wrappings above its shoulders. But the corpse kept clawing at him, groping for chinks in his armor. Brek knew that the fight could only end with either him or the mummy truly and completely dead.

As its dead hand blindly reached for him again, Brek swiped the warhammer sideways against the desiccated creature's elbow. The forearm broke away and hung by the wrappings. A succession of quick blows reduced the stumbling creature to a heap of feebly twitching bones and wrappings.

Ember zipped after Brek. She was glad for the dwarf's influence over the undead, but she wanted to deal with the monks herself. Without thinking about it, she selected an advancing red mask and ran at him full speed. Even among those of equal talent in the Order, Ember was known for her speed. Before her enemy quite knew where she was, she was hammering him with *shi kune*. He gasped and collapsed, but his friends were already drawing their net around Ember.

She jumped away from the first monk and whirled on the others, slipping between the sweeping hands of a scythelike strike. A back-kick tapped that man's head, sending him reeling. Two others closed in, spinning their own lethal kicks, but she rolled between them. A second later she was up and outside the broken ring. Two out of seven were dazed and stumbling.

Ember was barely set in her stance, *bahng ah jah se*, before three of the monks were on her. They tumbled forward in an impressive display of martial threat. She did not retreat; instead she leaped straight in the air at the last moment, scissoring her feet in a sharp arc that connected with the heads of two men. Using their heads as steps, she launched a spectacular flying elbow-strike against the third. The crack of her hardened joint against his skull dropped him instantly.

Two of the seven remained on their feet. The man she had attacked first with *shi kune* also was struggling back to his feet, but the others were clearly done.

From behind them, Sosfane yelled, "Get her, or your ineptitude will doom your souls before Nerull!"

Steeling themselves, they advanced. Ember smiled and crooked a finger.

Hennet stood half in the chamber, gazing in awe at Ember's martial display. At this rate, he thought, they'll all be dead before Nebin gets up his nerve! Then he noticed Aganon. As Sosfane angrily ordered her monks forward, Aganon's gaze narrowed on

Hennet, and the sorcerer glared back.

Aganon smirked and said, "Small world, no? I told you I would have my revenge. Now, I can simply kill you. Rules won't protect you here. I'll have the Duel Arcane trophy in the end."

He drew a pale wand from his shirt. It was thin but jagged, like a stylized bolt of lightning.

Hennet said nothing, but held forth his own wand. It was golden, and its light was not tainted by the evil illumination of the chamber.

"Another duel, then," the sorcerer said. "It will end the same way, except today you'll be losing your life along with the match."

Aganon sneered and brought up his weapon. The battle of wands was joined.

Nebin decided that Hennet could deal with Aganon; he had once before, after all. Brek was the one who needed aid. As he demolished the second mummy, the abyssal slug was already bearing down on the dwarf. Nebin raised his hands to fling a spell at the slug when three more red-masks sprinted into the chamber. All bore themselves like monks and moved to join those menacing Ember. She was already outnumbered, so Nebin turned to face them instead. He had to neutralize all three of them somehow. The gnome reviewed his magical arsenal.

When in doubt, stick with what you know, he decided.

Nebin gestured and uttered arcane syllables, manifesting a twisting pattern of subtle, shifting color directly in front of the red-masked men. One cenobite ran through it without noticing, but the other two stumbled to a stop, staring in complete fascination at the pattern.

I've snared you, you bastards! Nebin exulted.

He concentrated on the pattern, weaving it with new variations of color and complexity. The combinations thrilled him. A few greens, some purple. It was a sight to behold.

The red-mask who hadn't stopped hesitated when he found himself suddenly alone. Glancing around, he saw the gnome at the edge of the room. Nebin shrank back, frantically sputtering a spell of shielding as the cenobite charged him. The spell triggered just as a fist rocketed toward his face. Nebin squealed, his magical shield flared blue as it deflected the blow, and the red-mask yelped in pain over his broken knuckles.

"You know not who you face!" roared Nebin, trying to make himself sound intimidating as he groped for a scroll of staying, or his wand, or anything that could disable the attacker quickly.

The cenobite laughed grimly, then swept his leg out parallel to the floor, neatly tripping Nebin. The floor met the gnome's face with a sickening jolt. Nebin scrambled to roll over, and half succeeded before the red-mask struck again.

His hands whirled too quickly for the gnome to follow. Before Nebin really understood his peril, he was struck four times. For him, the battle was over.

Brek Gorunn swore. The damned slug was just looking at him. The dwarf gritted his teeth, anticipating anything.

It piped, "Flee, priest, unless you would die in a place where your pitiful god will not hear your screams."

As it spoke, the creature's eyes flared red. A compulsion washed over Brek Gorunn, pushing him to drop everything and flee to save his life. Gritting his teeth and groaning with the effort, he fought the urge. A cleric of the Dwarffather would not be bested by such a miserable trick! Brek had walked in many deep places of the world and faced real terrors unafraid; he would not run now, demon or no.

A red-mask hammered him from the side; the dwarf barely deflected the blows with his iron shield. Behind the cenobite lay Nebin's crumpled body. The dwarf looked away from the demon slug. There would be time enough to deal with the fiend after he showered the monk with the Dwarffather's "blessings."

The magical oil seemed almost to guide the hammer on its own and multiply the force of its blows. Instead of grasping the weapon by its handle, he gripped the stout leather thong and whirled it like a sling. The shrieking hammer was like a hurricane, threatening death at the slightest, glancing blow. Now it was Brek who advanced and his foe who was suddenly uncertain.

The red-mask impressed Brek with his bravery by deflecting the first three hammer blows, but deflecting a whirling hammer with a hand or elbow has its price. The cenobite tried to regain the initiative with a flurry of counterattacks, only to learn too late that his wrist and elbow were already shattered.

The dwarf growled from beneath his beard, "Your death god is weak!"

He pounded the sentiment home by bashing the man's face with his shield. Its clang against his skull was the last sound the cenobite ever heard.

Brek spun around, wondering where the abyssal child had gone.

Three cenobites lay senseless at Ember's feet. Three more maneuvered to renew their attack against her, calling out instructions to each other as they circled. Behind them, Sosfane watched, her eyes glittering. Ember had no time to wonder why Sosfane waited. The three cenobites rushed her with perfect timing.

Defiantly yelling, "For the Hand!" Ember pivoted on her heel thrust her palm into the first red-mask's neck.

Cartilage parted under her ferocious blow. Someone clubbed her but she feinted away, drawing her attackers on with her movement. Doubling back with a cartwheel kick, she caught a second under the chin. The impact was enough to hurl him backward, unconscious.

The last monk paused, taking stock, as Ember completed her cartwheel. More cautious with his own safety than his former compatriots had been, this one adopted a defensive posture. As Ember advanced, the cenobite retreated, step for step. Reluctant to expend time she might not have, Ember coiled her body, then thrust herself forward with both her fists out and together. Her full-body blow caught the last cenobite squarely on the chest. Ribs snapped, and the man fled, clutching his chest and gasping for breath.

Then there was only Sosfane. Ember knew that her friends still fought all around her, but it was the cult leader who represented the real threat.

She called out, "Are you afraid to face me, witch?"

The silver-haired woman smiled as she said, "You are a prodigy of my old Order and Kairoth's student. I'll enjoy killing you."

The sentence was barely complete when Sosfane leaped a dozen feet through the air like a bolt launched from a crossbow. A lethal high kick was aimed directly at Ember's chest. It would have struck her down if not for Loku's Bracers, which of their own accord, lifted Ember's arm and deflected the attack! Ember looked into her foe's eyes from a distance of barely a pace.

"*Your* order? The Enabled Hand never trained a foul creature like you!"

Ember kicked twice; both attacks were met by the woman's flashing wrists.

Sosfane lauughed and said, "I was a star pupil! Kairoth himself taught me the Order's most guarded techniques. The old fool didn't know I was also learning the secrets of the death god, Nerull! I reopened this temple years ago. Since then, I've been bending members of the Hand to Nerull's will, a few at a time. Some had to be forced, but not all. You would be surprised at how many were keen to join."

As she spoke, her hand crept into her sash. It lashed forth holding a small kama, its daggerlike blade tipped with a reddish liquid.

She jabbed at Ember, but the monk flipped back and kicked the kama from the tattooed woman's hand. It clattered to the ground, far out of reach.

Breathing hard, Ember exclaimed, "No one by the name of Sosfane was ever trained in the Order!"

"Adeva Silverhair was the name I used," said the woman, raining a flurry of blows on Ember. "But I am Sosfane, a disciple of the death god. "And when I've killed you," she gloated, "I shall feast on your flesh, in Nerull's name!"

They were upon each other again, trading blows, kicks, blocks, and throws too swiftly for any eye to follow. Training and instinct guided their hands and feet.

Ember stood toe to toe with her nemesis, and she knew Sosfane was beating her. Despite all her skill and noble purpose, Sosfane was simply more excellent. She was not really hurting Ember, yet.

Both knew the forms, the attacks, and the defenses. When Ember struck with *shi kune*, the stunning fist, Sosfane countered with *makee*, the blocking fist. Ember's *yup ju mok*, the hammer fist, was defeated by Sosfane's *pal moke makeei*, the outer forearm block.

Ember could find no way past Sosfane's defenses, and her own were likewise impenetrable. But Ember was growing tired. She had already fought seven men before facing Sosfane.

Again they drew apart for a heartbeat.

Sosfane said, "You are a high student of the Order, but your skills are stagnant. Nerull could teach you more . . . as he taught me."

Sosfane seemed to levitate into the air for a moment. Ember gasped—it was *soo jik so gee*, the vertical stance! This was far beyond her own skill—maybe even beyond Elder Kairoth's.

Sosfane unfolded from her superior aerial position, striking out with the side of her foot like a tornado brushing the ground. Unable to block, Ember took the full force of the blow. She tumbled and fell, feeling crippling pain shoot through her.

If there was ever a time for a hero, she thought, that time was now. Ember slipped a hand into her tunic and pulled out the vial she purchased at the Wizard's Hoard. She pulled the stopper with her teeth and gulped down the magical elixir.

At the liquid's first touch on her tongue, confidence coursed through her limbs and renewed strength pulsed in her hands. The sensation of power exceeded anything she could have imagined! She noticed that even Loku's Bracers pulsed with white light, in tune to her heartbeat. Somehow, the bracers were enhancing the effect of the elixir, and vice versa.

She slowly stood, and said, "Let's begin again."

Sosfane obliged.

Aganon was faster than Hennet. A blast of jagged light issued from the tip of his wand, searing toward Hennet with electrical fingers. Hennet held forth the Golden Wand. Its yellow glow intensified. With a clap like thunder, the golden light absorbed Aganon's electrical bolt. The wand sizzled and sparked in Hennet's hand, filled to capacity with its meal—tiny jolts of electricity discharged, stinging the sorcerer's hand. Hennet was thrilled.

He bore the pain from the sparks with a smile. After all, without his trophy, Aganon's first bolt might have simply killed him. Hennet could feel the force of the lightning bolt trapped within his wand. It raged like a caged beast, straining to break free.

Hennet mentally grasped that energy, molding and shaping it. This was not something he could normally do, he knew, but a power granted by the wand. When it was ready seconds later, he flicked it back at Aganon. This time, a golden beam of energy flowed between the two mages. Aganon tried to dodge, but a splash of golden fire enveloped him. He cried out in pain. Smoke rose from his clothing and his skin was charred, but he stood.

Hennet said, "Yield, or I'll burn you to a cinder!"

Brek looked wildly around for the abyssal child. Had it fled? He couldn't find it. Then his eyes fell on Nebin's body. When his attention was focused on the monk, the creature had decided to indulge its hunger on Nebin's defenseless form. Brek could easily see the slug's trail of slime on the floor. It pulled itself upright over Nebin and prepared to douse him with its digestive slime.

That's when Brek Gorunn threw himself bodily on the fiend, screaming, "Back to the Abyss with you, demon!"

The weight of the dwarf's body slammed the slug down and immediately dislodged it from the gnome. Brek grappled the rubbery flesh that burned his skin wherever they touched. The pair rolled away from the gnome, over and over. The creature screamed and spat its acid, but not a drop touched Nebin.

Brek Gorunn had saved Nebin's life. The dwarf took consolation in that knowledge as he rolled the demon farther from the gnome, as its acid burned away one of his hands, leaving a smoldering stump of liquid agony. With the one hand that remained to him, Brek strangled the horrid life from the demon's retching, shrieking, child's face—a life for a life, he grimaced.

Let Moradin be merciful when we meet.

Like all disciples of Sosfane, Aganon was accustomed to pain, but the blast from the Golden Wand hurt! He brought up his wand once more with shaking hands, then thought better of it. Up to that point he'd imagined the Golden Wand to be little more than a trinket. The realization that it was an item of real power unnerved him and left him badly hurt in the bargain.

He looked to Sosfane—she hammered Ember to the floor with an incredible aerial kick. It was only a matter of time before Sosfane crushed the Enabled Hand monk. If he ran from the conflict, Sosfane would find him and he would pay for his cowardice. That thought decided him; death here would be easier to endure.

Again Aganon discharged his wand. Searing lightning struck at Hennet. The sorcerer stood unflinching, as a mountain's summit weathers an electrical storm. This time, however, Hennet swung his wand like a club. When the wand struck Aganon's sizzling bolt, it reversed and streaked back at its caster.

This isn't fair, Aganon thought as the electricity tore into him.

His teeth sparked and his eyes burst. Through the pain, a vision of a skeletal hand appeared in his mind, reaching for him. He would have screamed, but the Reaper had his soul.

Ember launched herself from the ground at Sosfane, eschewing the time it would take to stand. Sosfane blocked the kick and Ember landed on her feet. The cultist thrust one hand forward attempting to clamp it around Ember's neck, but Ember ducked.

Charged with the combination of the elixir and Loku's Bracers, Ember launched four variations on standard kicks. She solidly struck her foe with *bitro cha gee*, the twisting kick, then again with *naeryo cha gee*, the downward kick. She had found a weakness in Sosfane's technique: too much reliance on the hand and fist, and too little on the foot!

"I have your measure, now. You won't knock me down again, Sosfane," promised Ember.

"We'll see."

Sosfane leaped into the air, out of Ember's reach, once more using the dreaded vertical stance.

She hovered, studying Ember, and said, "Now, it ends."

Sosfane prepared to descend on her foe like a falling star. Ember remembered the first kick and wondered whether she really could take another.

She braced for Sosfane's overwhelming kick, but it didn't come.

Sosfane floated, a dark angel surveying the carnage of the chamber, and screamed, "Where did you run to, rabbit!?"

Have her eyes failed her? wondered Ember. Then a memory flashed into her mind—Hennet during the final Duel Arcane had bested Aganon with a newly awakened spell of invisibility. She darted a glance over to Hennet. There was the sorcerer, standing over the smoking body of Aganon. He was looking at Sosfane, but met Ember's gaze for a heartbeat. He winked.

Ember knew the fight was hers. Hennet had turned her invisible.

Fuming and without a target, Sosfane alighted on the stone floor. Ember crept closer as Sosfane searched the chamber. The silver-haired fiend gasped aloud when she saw Aganon's smoking corpse.

Sosfane screamed at Hennet, "You should have fled with the rest. That error will cost you, as it has your companions."

Slowly she advanced on Hennet, still on guard lest the sorcerer cast some spell her way. Ember followed behind, unseen and unnoticed. She knew she could not allow Sosfane to reach the sorcerer—at close quarters, he would be helpless against her martial skill. And Hennet looked drained. Using the Golden Wand required a supreme effort of will. She saw him fumble for his crossbow. Sosfane continued advancing, taunting him.

"Soon, you'll keep Aganon company, a servant to usher Aganon into the deathless realm of Nerull."

Sosfane broke into a charge. Hennet got off a single bolt—it went wide—before the evil monk was upon him. He backed up and raised an arm. It was only luck that Sosfane's first kick broke his arm and not his neck. The sound of the crunching bone brought Ember's heart to her mouth.

Silently, she positioned herself behind Sosfane. Channeling all the remaining power from the magical potion into her hand, she struck a single blow. The strength of the potion and the desperate straits of herself and her friends combined and fueled her strength beyond any force she had known, and maybe ever would again. The sound of her open hand striking Sosfane's spine was thunderous. The black-hearted, rotten core at the center of the Order's disruption snapped backward soundlessly.

Sosfane was received directly into the kingdom of her evil god.

With Sosfane's passing, the shadow of her influence departed the temple. Where the shadow fled, those forced to take the Oath of Nerull were suddenly freed. They were left blinking and confused, as if suddenly wakened from an evil dream. In the city above, the vestige of Sosfane's influence melted like ice in the sun. Those who were only lightly touched, such as Elder Kairoth and some few others, suddenly walked easier, as if some burden, carried so long it was forgotten, was suddenly set aside.

A drawn-out, grating scream reverberated through the chamber where Ember stood triumphant. It came from the sick pool of light where demonic slugs swam in filth. Never clear, the vision faded completely, until only bare stone remained. With the passing of the window to the Abyss, the unclean illumination springing from every stone also dimmed, then failed. The chamber was quickly pulled into darkness, but wholesome, clean darkness was a great improvement.

From his position on the ground, Hennet groaned, "Are we victorious?"

All was hidden, without the light of evil illuminating the room. The sorcerer mumbled a simple spell of light—a flickering ghost-flame as bright as a candle answered his summons.

Ember, revealed in Hennet's light, smiled and said, "We are. Let's see to our companions."

Grimacing from the pain in his arm, Hennet stood. The small circle of light revealed Aganon, Sosfane, and just at the edge, Nebin's boot. None moved. Hennet and Ember rushed to where Nebin lay sprawled on his side.

Hennet checked for a pulse and was relieved to find it. He quickly retrieved one of his curative vials. Popping the cork, he dabbed the gnomes lips. Nebin's eyes slowly opened.

Hennet gave the gnome the rest to drink, saying, "You had me worried for a moment. I should have realized you're too ornery to die."

The magic was quick to work on Nebin, and he sat up, his bruises fading as Hennet watched.

The gnome said, "Did we win?"

Ember and Hennet laughed and Ember replied, "You and Hennet sound as if you have practice with that question. Come, we must see to Brek Gorunn."

Nebin climbed to his feet. Brushing off his coat, the gnome said, "One of the red masks knocked me senseless, but I could still make out what was going on. Brek knocked the cultist down, but the abyssal child was going to dissolve me! Thankfully, Brek pulled it away, right before I lost consciousness. He saved my life."

"I'll look," said Ember, and she moved off into the dark.

A few dozen feet away in the gloom Ember halted, looking at something on the floor ahead. Her body prevented the gnome from getting a clear view.

In a quiet voice, Ember said, "He died saving you, then."

"No, it can't be . . ." Nebin mumbled, stumbling forward. Hennet followed and saw that Ember spoke the truth. Brek had fallen. After his ferocious, grappling struggle with the abyssal child and its flesh-dissolving acids, little of the dwarf remained but bits of metal and hair. The demon, too, was slain, strangled by the dwarf's mighty sinews. But the creature's death came at too dear a price.

Nebin was speechless. Hennet put a hand on Ember's arm, tying to think of something he could say, some condolence he could offer. He had nothing. Ember cast a hand over her face. Though she made no sound, tears of terrible grief rolled down her cheek.

Brilliant sunlight did not allay the solemn mood in the courtyard. The Elders of the Enabled Hand stood assembled, their heads respectfully bowed. The courtyard, one of many contained in the Motherhouse, was reserved for monuments to heroes of the Order. And so it was offered to accept Brek Gorunn's remains.

Ember knelt before the small monument to the dwarf raised just that morning.

"Goodbye, Brek," she whispered. "I'm sorry."

She rested her hand for a moment on the cold stone, then rose to her feet. Behind her, Hennet stood, his face downturned. Nebin wept openly, clutching Brek's warhammer to his chest. Beyond the courtyard the banner of the Order flew at half mast. A deep bell tolled its grief.

Elder Kairoth stepped forward and spoke.

"Brek Gorunn returns to the halls of his fathers. He goes where gold, silver, and acclaim are of little worth, yet here his name shall long be spoken with hushed tones of respect. He died saving his friends from the fury of a beast most fell and the servitors of an evil god. His sacrifice ensured victory and life for his friends. Through their victory, our Order was rescued from a dark influence of secret evil; the death god's plans are laid bare and dissolved. Therefore, forevermore let the name of Brek Gorunn be remembered. He shall be entered in the sacred lists of the Order, and he will stand equal to Bezoar, Loku, and the other sacred heroes of the Enabled Hand. So let it be written; so let it be done!"

Nebin stepped forward and laid Brek's beloved warhammer across the monument.

"Well done," murmured Hennet. Ember nodded her agreement, holding the sorcerer's hand. Nebin stepped back, and all assembled regarded the monument until the bell tolled again.

After the ceremony was concluded, the companions followed the elders into the Motherhouse. They were ushered past lines of respectful novices into the elder's inner *dojo*. There, each was given a commendation for his part in saving the Order from Sosfane's machinations. Each was also awarded a small ribbon of silk. Elder Kairoth explained that each length of silk contained the strength of the Order woven into it. At need, the bearer could call on that strength in a desperate situation, or when grief grew too burdensome to bear alone.

All murmured their thanks, knowing the Order was doing them a great honor. But no honor, no matter how magnificent, could fill the hollow they felt in the centers of their chests. Their friend was dead.

Though the body of Brek Gorunn was gone, his memory remained anchored to the monument. His warhammer was his fiercest weapon and his tool of piety. In it, the dwarf invested much of his thought and purpose. In the years following, it was said that the hammer rang with the clamor of battle if danger threatened the Order, and the Motherhouse of the Enabled Hand was thus always forewarned of the approach of enemies.

Twelve days later, the three friends met one last time. They sat in the common room of the Cuttlestone, as they had often since Brek's memorial. They discussed many things sitting at this table, including what the future held for each of them. Hennet and Ember had also spoken privately of themselves. Heaping loss on grief, it became clear that he and Ember were destined to part. She wished to remain at the order, seeing to its renewal. Hennet couldn't fault her, but he wished with all his heart that she would join him on the road. Mostly, however, they spoke of their lost friend.

As the days of the season grew shorter, it was time for leave-taking.

"Ember, want to reconsider?" he joked, half-seriously. "On the morrow we must go. If you decide against remaining in New Koratia, you know I . . ." He couldn't continue. She already knew. She reached for his hand, saying nothing.

Hennet continued, "Nebin and I have long traveled together . . . he would welcome you as a companion, too. We could look out for each other. There are dangers in the world worse even than Sosfane, I imagine. And there is loneliness."

Ember shook her head.

"Dear Hennet," she said, gripping his hand harder, "I would come with you if I could—you know that—but there is much to do in the Order, to rebuild the damage done by Sosfane. I cannot leave now. I have made the only decision I can. I will stay with the Order until it is healed."

Hennet sighed, nodding glumly. With all their talk, he hadn't expected anything less. When he spoke of Nebin and himself as a team, he suspected that wouldn't last much longer, either. The College of Wizardry in New Koratia held a strong fascination for the gnome. Nebin spent many hours every night, after their talks in the Cuttlestone, reading in the college libraries.

As if in answer to Hennet's thought, the gnome cleared his throat. Nebin said, a plaintive note in his voice, "Hennet—I, too, must take my leave from your side for a while. I value your friendship more than gold, but I am summoned. The College of Wizardry here in New Koratia offered me a seat in a two-month course of study, 'The Metamagical Principle.' I have to accept, if I wish to advance in my craft. I should have spoken before."

The gnome hung his head, not meeting Hennet's gaze.

Hennet looked from Nebin to Ember, and shook his head. He had suspected, but all the words had been spoken, and there was no recalling them. Even he had a task that called him, else he would just stay with Ember.

Before coming to New Koratia, the winning of the Golden Wand in the Duel Arcane had been his only concern. With the Golden Wand hanging at his belt, new goals and broader concerns moved into the forefront of his mind. A sorcerer born, he couldn't gainsay his spirit of discovery.

"So, that's it," said Hennet. "Ember, of course the Order needs your strength right now. I apologize for bringing it up again. And, Nebin, you know I won't deny you this opportunity."

He paused, then continued. "I feel a summons, too. It's my legacy. Something in me yearns for the Far North, where the tribulations of dragons are rumored. Like you, Nebin, I can't resist seeing for myself the truth of my own heritage and power."

The sorcerer sat back, looking at his friends. Ember was closer than he ever could have hoped, while the gnome was more reserved after Brek's death, yet just as dear. Hennet fervently wished that Ember and Nebin would travel with him, despite his brave words to the contrary. He reflected on the nature of an adventurer, as he styled himself. It was dangerous, and lonely.

Though still new to the life, he realized that chance-met companions on the road were the only buffer against solitude. He desperately wished they could stay together, but they each had a separate path to follow.

So be it, he thought. What was the line the bards sang?

"Every good-bye is some tomorrow's hello."

R.A. Salvatore's
War of the Spider Queen

New York Times best-selling author R.A.
Salvatore, creator of the legendary dark elf
Drizzt Do'Urden, lends his creative genius to
a new FORGOTTEN REALMS® series that delves
deep into the mythic Underdark and even
deeper into the black hearts of the drow.

DISSOLUTION
Book I

Richard Lee Byers sets the stage as the delicate power structure
of Menzoberranzan tilts and threatens to smash apart. When
drow faces drow, only the strongest and most evil can survive.

INSURRECTION
Book II

Thomas M. Reid turns up the heat on the drow civil war and
sends the Underdark reeling into chaos. When a god goes silent,
what could possibly set things right?

December 2002

The latest collections from best-selling author R.A. Salvatore

Now available in paperback!

THE CLERIC QUINTET COLLECTOR'S EDITION

Follow the tales of scholar-priest Cadderly as he is torn from his quiet life at the Edificant Library to fulfill a heroic quest across the land of Faerûn. This one-volume collection includes all five of the original novels, complete and unabridged, and an introduction by R.A. Salvatore.

A new collectible boxed set!

THE ICEWIND DALE TRILOGY GIFT SET

A handsome hardside case houses the first three tales of Drizzt Do'Urden ever published – the novels that started it all! Follow the renegade dark elf and his companions as they pursue evil from the windswept reaches of Icewind Dale to the farthest edges of the desert. A must-have for any fan or collector.

All-new editions from
Margaret Weis &
Tracy Hickman

The Second Generation

Meet them again for the first time – the children of the
Heroes of the Lance, those who inherited the sword, the staff,
and the legacy of the heroes who came before them. This
all-new paperback edition features stunning cover art from
DRAGONLANCE® artist Matt Stawicki.

Dragons of Summer Flame

When the father of the gods returns to Krynn, the world
is shaken to its core. The battle that rages in this hottest of
summers will change the people and deities of Ansalon
forever. Striking cover art from Matt Stawicki graces this
all-new paperback edition!

Legends Trilogy Gift Set

A handsome hardcover case surrounds this trilogy of classic
titles from the foundation of the DRAGONLANCE saga. Each title
in this collectible boxed set features paintings by Matt Stawicki
and is a must-have for any DRAGONLANCE fan.

Revisit Krynn with these great collections!

An all-new anthology of classic
DRAGONLANCE® stories

The Best of Tales, Volume II

Edited by Margaret Weis & Tracy Hickman

This new collection contains a selection of classic DRAGONLANCE tales and an all-new roleplaying adventure by Tracy Hickman. This "best of" includes favorites by well-known DRAGONLANCE authors Douglas Niles, Richard A. Knaak, Paul B. Thompson & Tonya C. Cook, Dan Parkinson, Roger Moore, and others.

Available now!

The great modern fantasy epic —
now available in paperback

The Annotated Chronicles

Margaret Weis & Tracy Hickman

Margaret Weis & Tracy Hickman return to the Chronicles, adding notes and commentary in this annotated paperback edition of the three books that began the epic saga.

October 2002

Legend of the Five Rings™

Change is on the wind. . . .

The Four Winds Saga

Prelude
THE STEEL THRONE
Edward Bolme

The Empire teeters on the brink of disaster. To save his beloved realm, the emperor must make the ultimate sacrifice, entering the very realm of death. But in trying to save his people, he opens the door for his worst enemy to seize power.

First Scroll
WIND OF HONOR
Ree Soesbee

As the eldest child of the emperor, Tsudao's duty is clear—her life for the Empire, her sword for service, and honor above all. Now more than ever, her courage, her faith, and her integrity will be put to the ultimate test.

Second Scroll
WIND OF WAR
Jess Lebow

The forgotten son of the emperor, Akodo Kaneka is the most renowned warrior in all the lands. As the Empire spirals into chaos and the clans bicker among themselves, the forgotten son must find aid among the common people.

December 2002